The Twelve Days of Christmas
Stuart Weatherby

Weatherby Publishing Ltd.

First Published in 2010 by Weatherby Publishing Ltd.

A CIP catalogue record for this title is available from the British Library
ISBN 978-0-9564277-0-0

Printed in the UK by CPI Cox & Wyman, Reading, RG1 8EX
Weatherby Publishing Ltd
www.weatherbypublishing.com

Contents

Part One   Tom Kruise with a K   On the first day of Christmas my
                                       true love sent to me...
Chapter 1   Christmas Day   One present, repeated   9
Chapter 2   Boxing Day   Two goals for granddad   20
Chapter 3   The day after Boxing Day Three damaged dryers   31
Chapter 4   28th December   Four reasons to meet   42
Chapter 5   29th December   Five minutes late   52
Chapter 6   30th December   Six sayings you won't forget   60

Part Two   Dennis Malcolm Leslie Johnston

Chapter 1   Christmas Day   One oversized microwave   73
Chapter 2   Boxing Day   Two disastrous goals   81
Chapter 3   The day after Boxing Day Three tears of sadness   93
Chapter 4   28th December   Four American tourists   102
Chapter 5   29th December   Five gold scams   112
Chapter 6   30th December   Six double whiskeys   121

Part Three Tom and Den

Chapter 1   New Year's Eve   Seven hours in prison   133
Chapter 2   New Year's Day   Eight Christmas hymns   151
Chapter 3   2nd January   Nine wasted years   163
Chapter 4   3rd January   Ten heartfelt sorrys   180
Chapter 5   4th January   Eleven other victims   195
Chapter 6   5th January   Twelve reasons why   213

EPILOGUE – Sometimes in life, you get what you want   224

This book is dedicated to my wife Melanie and my daughter Amelia Rose. Without my wife's love, help and understanding this book would not have been possible

In loving memory of my father, my Uncle Derek, Majo and Mollie

Acknowledgements

Without the love and support of those people around me, the journey to finishing my book would have been a very difficult one indeed. So I would like to take this opportunity to thank those family members and friends who were there when I needed them the most: in my hour of need. I would also like to give a special mention to those who contributed directly to my book's creation. If it wasn't for them the final version would not be as good as it is. Steve and Aisling Logan, who generously gave their time and resources to help my wife and myself create the front cover and to typeset the document. Tracy Tabak who helped to finish off the front cover, providing the all important missing piece and who put together a great advertisement. Roger Savage whose proofing skills were provided when the clock was ticking down and who was there to give me advice. Finally to Mark Stephens who made a very helpful initial proof several years ago. Thank you to you all.

Part One
Tom Kruise with a 'K'

Chapter 1
Christmas Day – one present, repeated

Tom used to like Christmas, but that was a long time ago. He knew exactly when the magic went, but it was a day, to be honest, that he'd rather forget. Now that he's hit the ripe old age of thirty-four, he's about as cynical as you can get, and to him it seemed like a commercial binge on the grandest of scales. Prepare to do battle in the shops of Great Britain for presents that either you'd buy for yourself or that are completely pointless and sit idle, cluttering up your undersized London flat. Having said that, Tom's disgruntled state may have had a lot more to do with the fact that he felt he hadn't exactly made a roaring success of his time on the planet. Unless you regard losing your girlfriend to someone else and running your business at a substantial loss, as hitting the big time.

These thoughts were whizzing through his mind the whole of his Christmas Day car journey, occasionally interrupted by the booming voice of his mother, Sergeant Major Veronica.

"Bring Albert back by thirteen hundred hours. Any later and you'll be peeling potatoes for the rest of your miserable life, do you hear me, soldier?"

"Sir, yes sir," Tom imagined himself saying, standing to attention while saluting his mum.

When Tom finally arrived at his granddad's village, it was ten minutes to one and he was due back at one on the dot. You've got no chance of that happening, he thought to himself. After finding a parking space outside the pub with relative ease and saving himself a few valuable minutes, he quickly made his way down a quiet pedestrian path, past the local Italian restaurant to a small parade of cottages. As he approached the front door of the one nearest the lane, his hand poised to knock, it swung open.

"She's going to poison the turkey, you know that don't you," said granddad Albert, with a cheeky grin on his face.

"Merry Christmas granddad."

"And a very Merry Christmas to you Tom," Albert replied. "Now I thought that you could blame it on me. I don't know, we could say I lost my reading glasses. What do you think?"

"You don't have any reading glasses," Tom said breaking into a smile.

"Well spotted," Albert said, smiling back.

"Look, before we rush off I wondered if you wanted to try a little sipper, last year's sloe gin. I like to put some by for special occasions." Tom didn't want to say no despite the time constraints because the truth was, he would much rather spend time with his granddad than be back with his parents.

"...and it wouldn't be the same, of course, if we didn't have a piece of this Roquefort cheese that I've had under wraps for a few days. Look at that," he said, grabbing the handle of a large silver dome serving top, positioned on the edge of a circular kitchen table. When he lifted it up it filled the air with the most pungent of odours. The smile on his rugged and worn face illustrated a strange sense of excitement about what many people may perceive to be a glass of strong syrupy liquid and a piece of over ripe cheese.

"Right, if there's anything you need to tell me, that you can't say in front of your mum, now's your chance," he said getting straight to the point. "You know apart from the Chloe thing."

"Why? Do I look worried?"

"Well my dear boy, if I'm honest it's written all over your face," the older man said. "You look like so many youngsters these days, who spend their free time trying to escape from the burdens of life. Walking around with the weight of the world on their shoulders." As he talked, Albert poured some of the maroon coloured liquid into a tiny glass he'd placed in front of Tom.

"It looks like I might lose my business."

"My God, it really hasn't been your year. They say it comes in threes you know, bad luck. Anyhow, sorry to interrupt, carry on."

"I had a meeting a couple of days ago, with my accountant."

"What, the one you don't like, a bit shifty?"

"Yep that's him, and my business partner Raymond."

"And…"

"The long and the short of it is, the credit crunch is starting to hit my business. People can't afford to buy as many paintings and we're in debt to the tune of fifty thousand pounds, give or take the price of a cheap package holiday." Albert whistled in recognition of the large amount involved.

"Do you need some money?" This was Albert's first thought and that was why Tom felt so comfortable confiding in him. There was never any judgment, or criticism, just support. "I've got a little stash going on under the mattress for a rainy day, if you'd like."

"That's very kind of you but this was only a cunning plan to find out where you'd hidden it. No, only kidding. Thanks but I need to seriously consider whether or not it's worth throwing good money after bad, if you know what I mean."

"What are your options?"

"Well Raymond wants out. Declare bankruptcy and go our separate ways."

"Sounds like you've got another separation on your hands."

"This year won't be going down as a golden one in the Kruise memoirs, that's for sure."

"No, no it won't." As Albert said this his eyes glazed over and filled up with water.

"Oh God I'm sorry," Tom said, immediately feeling bad for his oversight.

"That's alright, it's not your fault. I just can't seem to stop myself from missing her. I still can't believe she's gone. She loved Christmas, you know, more than any other time of the year."

"Yes I know. Remember when I used to come over and stay with the two of you. We'd listen to Nat King Cole records on that old stereo of yours. Grandma would bake her homemade mince pies and fruit loaf. That really was the best fruit loaf."

"It was, and I'd borrow Frank's van and go down the yard round the back of Eltham parade," Albert said, before blowing his nose on his hanky. "We'd take ages picking a tree, checking each of them over to find the right one. Your grandma would spend weeks before Christmas making new decorations. Do you remember when we lived in Blackheath? On Christmas Eve we'd take you to the high street and wait for the brass band to arrive."

"How could I forget? And we'd sing carols until we were so cold our feet would be like ice blocks." But Tom was lying: he tried not to think of those days, as if he'd locked them away in some dark compartment in his mind and thrown away the key, only for it to be prised open by his granddad's comment. Now it was Tom's turn as his eyes glazed over recalling the sight of his little sister, Jessica, with a big grin on her face that seemed to stretch from one ear to the other.

"Anyhow, less of this sentimental stuff," said Albert blowing his nose one last time. "It's twenty past one, what excuse are we going to give your mother?"

"We could tell her the traffic was bad?"

"Well, I'm not sure she'll believe us," Albert replied gently shaking his head. "Everyone knows it's about the only day of the year when the roads are clear. And anyway what have I told you about lying?"

"I don't know, don't do it?"

"Well obviously only do it under extraordinary circumstances. No Tom. If you're going to lie, lie big. Make it as far fetched as you possibly can, that way people are much more likely to believe you."

"We could always tell her the truth." They looked at each other, and in a moment that made them both laugh out loud, they shook their heads and said in unison:

"Bad idea."

*

"…so anyway, it took quite a while but I managed to persuade granddad not to call the police. The trouble was, in return, I had to agree that we'd wait until he was convinced that the spaceship wasn't hovering above his cottage anymore. So I'm really sorry we were late mum but I didn't know what else to do," Tom said trying to look as serious as possible.

"Do you think we should get some sort of help for him?" asked Tom's mother, lowering her voice in a conspiratorial way.

"I think I'd leave it for a while. It could just be a phase he's going through," Tom said biting his bottom lip. "He probably does it for attention you know, now that grandma's gone."

"True, true, yes I can see why that would be the case," Veronica whispered while stirring the gravy. "Anyway lunch is nearly ready, why don't you make yourself useful and get everyone to sit down at the dining room table for me, there's a good boy. Oh and ask your father to come and give me a hand carving the turkey."

Tom obediently trooped off to the lounge, where his younger sister Rebecca, his father Jeff, his grandmother Petula, and his granddad were in the middle of a conversation.

"…so have you done anything naughty recently nan?" asked Rebecca, knowing her grandmother could be a bit mischievous at times.

"Nothing for a while," Petula replied looking a bit disappointed with herself; but a moment later a big smile appeared across her face.

"Well there was one thing. Jeff do you remember Ivy from around the corner?"

"What Ivy, as in Stan and Ivy?"

"That's right, course Stan's dead now God rest his soul. Well she does go on, sometimes on the phone, you know what I mean. It's as if she doesn't have to come up for air. Anyway, a couple of weeks back, after she'd been talking for about half an hour, basically about herself, well, I rang the door bell."

"No way," said Rebecca putting her hand over her mouth in mock horror.

"What, and pretended someone was at the door?" asked Tom. Petula nodded, with an expression on her face of a school girl who'd just been caught doing something they shouldn't.

"Nan you're so naughty," commented Rebecca.

"That's not all. If I see her coming down the road, you know from the front living room...," she said chuckling to herself, "...I put my coat on and pretend I'm about to go out."

"Oh my God, Petula. That's outrageous," Jeff said, laughing so much he had to put his drink down.

"Alright less of this Christmas fun, before I forget dinner is about to be served" said Tom trying to bring the group back to the business at hand. "Dad, mum requests your turkey carving skills in the kitchen if you don't mind. The rest of you rabble, off to the dining room please," commanded Tom.

"Tom," whispered Rebecca as they settled themselves down at the table. "Before I forget, what did you get mum for Christmas?"

"Why? It's a bit late now isn't it?"

"Come on just tell me otherwise I won't be able to relax properly."

"I got her what she's been hinting at for like the last month. A foot spa."

"Oh, no. I assumed that you'd get that gardening stuff". As she said it, Rebecca looked up to see Albert staring at both of them with a playful expression on his face.

"What have I always told you, when you assume it makes an ass out of you and me," Albert said offering them both an olive.

"Yes, thanks for that, but what are we going to do, we're in so much trouble," Rebecca said trying not to laugh.

"What are you going to do?" said Tom, giving his sister a gentle push on her shoulder.

"What are we all going to do?" Albert said beaming back.

"What? Not you as well?"

"I'm afraid so. Well she did go on didn't she. I guess there's not a lot we can do, let's just hope she sees the funny side of it. After all it's the giving not the receiving, right?" Albert said shrugging his shoulders.

"Ok, everyone for turkey breast," announced Tom's dad as he appeared in the doorway between the kitchen and the dining room.

"Can I have a leg, please," called out Tom. They were soon joined at the table by Tom's mum and dad. Silence then descended for a few moments while everyone concentrated on dishing out the various parts of the Christmas dinner.

"So how's Chloe these days?" asked Tom's mum. Her question almost made Tom choke on his turkey leg.

"Oh she's fine. Well I mean she's not fine, but she's much better than she has been for a long time and the doctors are confident she will make a full recovery in the next couple of months."

"Do they know what's wrong with her?" asked his dad.

"Well they think it may be a problem with her thyroids," Tom explained gesturing to several different parts of his body in the hope that one of them would be right.

"I had a similar thing when I was her age," said Petula. "Hurt myself playing tennis. You know I couldn't walk properly for months afterwards. That was before I met your grandfather, of course. I was a bit useful back then, especially at the old forehand volley."

"Oh right," Tom said politely, knowing that his nan could get the wrong end of the stick sometimes.

"Well tell her to come and see us as soon as she's well enough, it's been ages," said his mum.

"Over a year now actually," commented Rebecca. Knowing his sister as well as he does, it wouldn't have surprised Tom if her comment was aimed at putting the cat amongst the pigeons.

"Has it really, doesn't time go by so quickly," said Veronica.

"And what about your work, still selling loads of paintings I hope." As Tom looked up to answer the question, he caught his granddad looking back at him.

"It's, errh, fine at the moment, a little bit slower than last year."

"I still can't believe it, our son running his own successful chain of galleries."

"It's not that impressive," said Tom, trying to play it down.

"Well I hope you don't mind but I've told all the neighbours about your business venture."

"What about you Veronica, how's the charity work going?" Albert asked, trying to deflect the attention away from his squirming grandson.

"It's going really well, actually. We managed to raise over £10,000 for the local church roof and then another £5,000 for the Emily Ash Cancer Trust. The only trouble is my feet are killing me at the moment. All that walking about, I could really do with a foot spa." All of a sudden the room went quiet and the only sound that could be heard was of roast potatoes being nervously shuffled around dinner plates.

*

"Come on Veronica, why don't you come through and play a game with everyone."

Rebecca was standing by the stereo. She'd turned the music down so she could make out the conversation between her mum and dad, who were sitting next door in the dining room.

"I told you, I don't feel well. I've got a headache," said Veronica, the sound of her voice was faint and could only just be made out.

"Ask her if she wants to use a foot spa to help her relax," whispered Albert.

Tom went to laugh out loud but when he tried to hold it in, began to choke. After several liqueurs they were all starting to see the funny side of it. Everyone that was except for Tom's mum.

"I'll take you shopping in the sales if you want."

"Good idea dad, go for the bribery," commented Rebecca.

"What, to Selfridges?" Veronica said, her voice softening considerably.

"If you want to go to Selfridges, then yes, we'll go to Selfridges," said Jeff in a soothing voice,

"What, and I can buy what I want?"

"Yes…" Jeff said without hesitation, "…whatever you want." Sensing that her parents' conversation was coming to an end, Rebecca wisely drowned out their voices by turning the music back up. A few moments later Veronica and Jeff walked back into the lounge. Jeff was clutching a box which had Trivial Pursuit written on the side of it.

"Trivia everyone," said Jeff, as if the whole scene that his wife had just caused over the three identical Christmas presents she'd been given, had never happened.

"Sounds great," Tom said like an over enthusiastic school boy.

"What about teams?" asked Rebecca. "We could split people up by age? The youngest in one team, then the second youngest in the other and so on."

"That means I'd have to go with Tom," said Veronica sharply. Tom didn't respond to his mum's venomous attitude.

"Ok, what about boys versus girls?" Rebecca asked.

"Fine," said Veronica, failing to look interested. Tom and Rebecca quickly cleared a space on the coffee table and helped each other set up the board.

"Pink versus blue would be appropriate, I think. Any objections?" Rebecca asked looking at her mother, who shook her head. "Right, throw the dice granddad, highest starts."

"Five, not bad. Now you have a go nan," directed Rebecca.

"Six, well done, girls to start. Throw again nan. A four, ok well at this stage you can have whatever you want."

"I don't mind. What about entertainment, if that's ok with everyone?" said Petula.

"Are you ready?" said Jeff. "I can't believe how easy this is."

"Come on get on with it dad," said Rebecca impatiently.

"Which international organisation tried to sue the Village People in 1979?"

"Oh I know," said Petula getting excited, "Pembury Horse and Hound club."

"Is that your final answer?" asked Jeff, teasing them.

"No its not dad, don't be mean," said Rebecca giving him a wry smile to indicate that she wasn't going to tolerate such tactics. "It's an international organisation, nan, and I think the question is referring to the band called the Village People. You know the ones that dressed up in different costumes like a policeman and a red indian. I think the answer is the YMCA."

"Correct."

"Sorry dear, I got a bit confused. I could have sworn they sued the County Council, you know over the incident with the Basset hounds. Terrible that was, not sure that those poor dogs will ever be the same again."

"That's ok nan, you throw again. Two well done, for a piece of cheese."

"Brown, ok that's art and literature. Now this is a bit trickier. Which Irish winner of the Nobel Prize for Literature was a member of the French Resistance?"

"That is so hard, I haven't got a clue. What about you, mum?" asked Rebecca.

"Nope."

"Nan?"

"Well, I think I might know." At this point the expressions of the men changed from one of frustration to opportunity, as they were itching to get into the game. Albert sat impatiently shaking the die in his right hand.

"I think its Beckett," said Petula looking unsure.

"You'll have to be more specific."

"Dad," said Rebecca, in an 'I've warned you once before kind of way.'

"Samuel Beckett."

"Is the right answer. How do you know that?" Jeff asked in disbelief.

"I don't know really, I just do."

"Throw again, nan," said Rebecca handing her the die.

"Four, so that's Sport or Entertainment."

"Entertainment, seems to be lucky for us so far."

"Is it alright if I ask this one dad?" enquired Tom.

"Yes of course, here you go," said Jeff passing over the box of question cards.

"Which famous comedian died on stage in…" Tom stopped abruptly. He had a distressed look on his face.

"Come on finish the question," said Veronica.

"…1984."

Veronica then gave Tom the bitterest of stares that would have turned most mortals into a pillar of salt, before her bottom lip started to quiver.

"You, you, you…" she said before the tears welled up in her eyes. She then got up and ran out of the room. There was a hushed awkward silence. Tom could feel his heart pounding in his chest and his mind saying over and over, 'I'm sorry it was my fault, I'm sorry it was my fault, I'm sorry it was my fault.'

Chapter 2
Boxing Day – two goals for granddad

"So how was Christmas Day?" Duncan asked, just before he took a large bite out of the double bacon cheeseburger he'd bought in the station. They were sitting opposite each other in a set of four seats on the 1:20pm train out of Liverpool Street Station, heading towards White Hart Lane.

"That stinks. It's making me feel sick."

"Oh, I'm sorry. Is it bothering you?" said Duncan as he waved the burger in front of Tom's face.

"Get it away from me."

"Come on don't be such a woman."

"If I'm a woman then what does that make you? All I can say is that someone who uses lip balm on a regular basis needs to be a bit more careful about making those sorts of accusations. Anyway, Christmas Day..." Tom said holding his hand in front of his nose, "...yes I'm glad you asked. It was an unmitigated disaster, the kind that is truly representative of my life at the moment."

"Why?" Duncan said trying to speak with a mouthful of half chewed burger.

"Because me, my sister and my granddad all bought my mum the same stupid Christmas present and she got the right royal hump."

"Ha," Duncan said spraying out a piece of lettuce from his half opened mouth, which missed Tom's jeans by a cat's whisker and ended up getting stuck on the floor of the train.

"What was it?"

"A foot spa."

"That's alright, she could have one for each foot and one spare for, I don't know, special occasions."

"Damn."

"What?"

"If only you'd been there, you could have made the situation a whole lot better."

"It reminds me of one year when I left it to the last minute to get my parents a present. All I could find was a lava lamp. You should have seen their faces, it was priceless."

"What about you? How was your Christmas?" Tom said, ignoring his friend's inappropriate quip and quickly moving the conversation on.

"Same old story really. Mum cremated the turkey. I mean it was edible but only just. Nan fell asleep. I got really drunk. Dad gave me a lecture on the importance of being honest. Call me Einstein but I think he was trying to indirectly imply that I'd been a bit dishonest in the past."

"Oh, really? While we're on the subject did you ever own up to starting the fire, the one which burnt down your parents' shed."

"Course not. I mean, it was an accident," Duncan said. "I definitely put that cigarette out. Definitely."

"What else could it have been?"

"I don't know, do I?"

"What did you say it was?"

"I didn't say it was anything, they don't even know I smoke."

"And there rests the case for the prosecution, my Lord. My own observation is that you are in fact subconsciously aware of your own guilt and this is driving you to a life of comfort eating and binge drinking."

"Don't talk to me about morality. Have you told your parents you've split up with your girlfriend yet?" As Duncan asked this, his words became hard to make out above the electronic beeping noise as the doors slid shut. The train then juddered into action as the driver tentatively pulled away.

"No, not yet." Tom said looking out the window.

"And why's that?" Duncan asked, tucking into a chocolate bar he'd recently liberated from his jacket pocket.

"I suppose there's always been a part of me that thinks she'll come back."

"Mate there's more chance of me, I don't know, winning a Pulitzer Prize than there is of that happening."

"I'd be amazed if you ever won a pub prize to honest. Even if the winner was the person who can eat and drink the most and projectile vomit the furthest. But thanks for those kind words of comfort. I feel like a great weight's been lifted from my shoulders," Tom replied sharply, clearly reflecting the fact that Duncan's words had struck a nerve.

"What? I'm only trying to be realistic. Hello, earth calling Major Tom, come in Tom. Spaceship Chloe embarked on a journey for some other planet a long time ago, pal. That's life. Come on, trust me, you're better off without her."

"Right, that's all very helpful. Does that mean, in your infinite wisdom, that you know something that I don't know then?"

"What do you mean? I don't know anything more than she went off with some guy, last Christmas Eve."

"What and you don't know who he is?"

"No, of course not. What kind of a person do you think I am? Do you think I would withhold such important information?" Duncan said looking unconvincingly disgusted.

"Yes actually, you just told me that you're the kind of person that would lie to his parents, you doughnut."

"Talk about the pot calling the kettle black" but before Duncan could start a lengthy argument, Tom's mobile phone started ringing,

"Da…da da dah…da da dah…der der der der derh…da…da da dah…da da dah…der der der der derh…"

"Hello. Hi, dad. What? No, I don't, yes, yes of course. Oh no, I don't believe it. Yes, of course I will. No, no I understand. Oh my God. I just can't believe it. It's such a shock. How did it happen? Right. I don't know what to say. I'm with Duncan, we're on our way to the match. What happens now? Yes, right, ok. We'll talk later. Ok. Bye."

"What's wrong mate, you look like you've just seen an ugly bird?" Duncan said half-laughing, half-snorting.

"It's my granddad, he's, well, he died, about an hour ago."

"I'm so sorry mate. What happened?"

"The emergency services tried to resuscitate him but he didn't respond. They said his heart gave out."

"Mate, that's terrible. Look, I'd understand it if you don't want to go to the match."

"No it's alright, it's alright. You know he was a Spurs fan. He would have wanted me to go along. I think it's the right thing to do."

"That's such a shock. I remember when my granddad died, over fifteen, yeah over fifteen years ago now," said Duncan. He looked like he wanted to say a lot more but instead he sat staring at Tom with a dazed expression on his face, waiting for him to say the next word.

"My granddad was such a good bloke," Tom eventually said, looking around him. "You know my nan died last year. Dad just said he thinks granddad died of a broken heart. He's probably right you know, that's what happened, he probably died of a broken heart."

*

The referee had just blown his whistle to signal the end of the first half.

THE TWELVE DAYS OF CHRISTMAS

"A goal down, just before half time, the dirty cheating Arsenal," Duncan said, pushing his hand away in disgust. "It was definitely offside."

But Tom wasn't listening. He was physically there, in the stadium, but emotionally and mentally he was in his grandparents' back garden; playing football when he was ten years old.

"So who's the greatest football team in the world," promoted Albert.

"England."

"Ok, good answer. We'll try again. Who's the greatest club team in the world?"

"Tottenham Hotspur."

"Correct and what are we going to do on Saturday?"

"We're going to beat Arsenal at the lane."

"That's right, so sing along with me."

"We're going to beat the Arsenal at the lane, we're going to beat the Arsenal, going to beat the Arsenal, we're going to…" sung Albert, whilst doing a sort of jig and dribbling with the football at the same time.

"Albert, leave the poor boy alone," shouted Tom's nan through the kitchen window. Tom never forgot that moment, because Albert shouted back "he's alright, we're just having a laugh." Then he waited until she wasn't looking and pulled out a small magazine from the back pocket of his baggy trousers, bent down and said,

"I want you to have this." At the time Tom didn't comprehend the true significance of his granddad's gesture. He'd handed him a copy of the 1981 FA cup final replay programme.

"Wow that's great. Thanks granddad."

"Now do you remember why this was such a great match?"

"Ricki Villa scored the best goal ever."

"That's right son," Albert said looking at him through watery eyes. "Now I'm not the type to ever tell you what you should do with your life or what sort of person you should be. I'll leave that up to you. Just remember never to forget who you are and where you came from.

Most importantly of all, that you're a good person."

"I won't granddad."

"Coming for a beer? I said are you coming for a beer."

"What, beer? Yeah. Yeah, coming." Tom was suddenly brought back into the present by Duncan's hand on his shoulder. They quickly jostled their way to the bar, waited for a few minutes and got served with two pints of lager. They then retreated to a quiet corner to have a quick chat.

"How're you feeling?"

"I'm in shock to be honest, one nil down at half time. I mean the goal was definitely offside. The linesman wasn't much passed the halfway line."

"Yeah, no, I mean about your granddad."

"Oh. I don't know, really. It hasn't sunk in. We were close, you know, it was like he was my mate. He was one of life's characters, one of life's gentlemen. He loved grandma, he thought the world of her and when she died I guess a part of him died with her. How do you replace the irreplaceable?"

"I don't know but I feel like replacing our right-back at the moment, he's playing like a pansy. Why can't he just hoof the ball into row Z rather than trying to get his body in the way all the time?" Duncan finished his comment off by demonstrating the actions of a player booting the ball into the top of the stand.

"Come on let's finish these and go back for the second half turn-around, as if," Duncan added.

Despite their reservations, there was a marked improvement in Tottenham's second half performance, which culminated in a goal in the seventy-eighth minute. It set up a nail biting last ten minutes. Arsenal posed a constant threat throughout the second half but just couldn't make their dominance pay.

"Oh no, he's clean through, I can't watch," said Duncan putting his hands over his eyes, as the Arsenal striker charged into the penalty box unchallenged.

"He's chipped the keeper..." Tom said, giving his friend a running commentary, "...and, and, he's hit the cross bar. The ball's bounced off the beautiful, thick, sturdy, fantastic woodwork." Both of them were so relieved they felt like they'd just scored. There were just two minutes of regular time left plus two minutes of injury time added on.

"Come on do it for granddad," Tom whispered. As soon as he said this his eyes filled with tears and his heart felt like someone had stabbed a knife straight through the middle of it. At that moment it dawned on him that the person he loved more than anyone in the world, was gone forever. No more Sunday football round at his cottage. No more going out in the freezing cold to pick Christmas trees together. No more complaining about Tom's mum but, more than all of that, no one he could talk to about how he really felt; about things that were important to him.

"Go on, pass the ball, pass, shoot, shoot, yes, you beauty, you beauty," shouted Duncan, as Tottenham scored a second goal to go in the lead. They put an arm around one another and jumped up and down, punching their fists in the air. A surge of emotion bought another tear to Tom's eye. He rubbed his cheek on the shoulder of his jacket to stop it from streaming down his face. No one noticed though because the Spurs supporters were too busy celebrating.

'If only my granddad was here'. As this thought popped into his head Tom felt a presence; as if something moved through his body. It made him shiver but he wasn't cold, quite the opposite in fact. As things calmed down, he took a long look round the ground. For a moment everything went silent. When his eyes came into focus, he could have sworn he saw his granddad several rows down, in the crowd. He had a huge grin on his face which stretched from ear to ear, and he was holding his arms at right angles and moving them up and down, doing his funny jig.

*

Tom gingerly pulled himself up off the sofa in his living room and went into the kitchen. He unscrewed the top of a half empty bottle of vodka that was sitting on the black marble designer worktop and poured a generous measure of the potent liquid into a cloudy glass. He lethargically made his way over to the fridge. As he prised the door open he was propelled back by an overpowering odour of unknown origin. He quickly searched its hidden depths while holding his breath and found an unopened, but on closer inspection past its sell-by-date, carton of tropical fruit juice. He muttered to himself that it was better than nothing. Tom desperately needed to talk to someone. He tried phoning his friend Rick but all he got was his answer machine.

"I'm out right now, probably having a great time. Don't worry that you haven't caught me, if you leave a 'massage' after the tone I'll get back to you pronto. Ciao. Beep."

Christ he could be such an idiot sometimes, thought Tom. Perhaps it was for the best. What sort of sensible advice are you going to get from someone who says 'leave a massage'. He sat back down on his cream sofa, staring at the space in front of him.

Suddenly, the noise of the phone made Tom jump. Perversely, after wishing all evening that someone would call him, when they finally did, he felt anti-social. After several rings he managed to convince himself that he was only delaying the inevitable and didn't want the stress of having to remember to call someone back.

"Hello."

"Hi Tom."

"Dad, how are you feeling'?" Tom asked, trying to sound attentive even though he was tired and the alcohol had made him a little fuzzy headed.

"So so, not sure it's sunk in yet."

"I know what you mean."

"Good result today."

"Yes, yes granddad would have been pleased."

"You're right he would." There was an awkward pause.

"Sorry about your mother yesterday."

"Let's not talk about it, alright."

"She doesn't mean what she says sometimes."

"You could have fooled me." This time there was an even bigger lull in the conversation.

"Well I just phoned you up to tell you that granddad left you and Rebecca some money."

"Really, I wasn't expecting that."

"Well he wasn't joking every time he said he had some money hidden under his mattress."

"Damn I always thought he was bluffing. I knew I should have searched his bedroom."

"Yes he was quite good with money. He left you £10,000 each."

"Right."

"Just thought you should know."

"No, thanks dad."

"I know it can't replace him."

"It's ok dad."

"Anyway, got a few things I need to be getting on with. I'll give you a call about the funeral, as soon as we know."

"Ok, and dad."

"Yes son."

"Oh, no it's ok. It's nothing."

"Ok we'll talk soon."

"Take care,"

"You too." His dad hung up and after staring at the phone for a few minutes, Tom got up and poured himself another full measure of vodka before falling back down on the sofa. At several points in the evening he tried to distract himself. First, by playing the football game on his console. When it took him what seemed like an eternity just to get a shot on goal, he gave up. He then got an obsessive desire to cut his nails and began searching the top two drawers of his wooden chest for a pair of nail scissors. They were such a mess, he thought that, given the fact he had nothing better to do, he would tidy them up. After pulling the first one out, he emptied its contents on his bed. In between the old receipts and junk, he found some photographs. There was a pile of them; different shapes and sizes, held together by an ill fitting elastic band.

The first one he looked at showed his ex-girlfriend, Chloe, sitting in the middle of his two friends Rick and Duncan in a bar in Ibiza. She looked beautiful; her long blond hair cascading over her shoulders, her white teeth accentuating her deep tan. It brought back some bad memories though. Tom ate something that disagreed with him on the first day and spent most of the week in bed, while Chloe hung out with his friends.

The next photo was of them on the sofa at his parents' house. It was their first Christmas together. They'd been seeing each other for nearly a year. To celebrate, he'd decided to go out and buy a real Christmas tree; the biggest one that would fit in his new flat, which he'd only bought a few months before. As a surprise he'd made a loose arrangement for an evening in with Chloe, which he hoped would include decorating their new tree and generally getting in the Christmas mood. He'd bought mince pies, a turkey curry, some mini Christmas puds, a compilation Christmas CD, a few bottles of red wine—Merlot, her favourite—and a pair of Santa hats which had a small button on the side. When you flicked it, four red stars on the front would light up in sequence.

Tom had this vivid memory of sitting on the sofa, wearing one of the Santa hats with the lights flashing, finishing off a bottle of red wine. He then fell asleep before she finally texted him back in the early hours of the morning, to tell him she wasn't going to be able to make it.

He took another large gulp of his drink. The vodka was so strong it stung the back of his throat and made him cough a little. Looking at the old photographs was making him feel even more depressed, so he put them on the side table next to the bed and then stuffed everything else back in the drawer. It looked even more untidy than when he first started.

He went back into the lounge, slumped on the sofa and switched the TV on. After flicking through the same channels a number of times, he finally settled on watching the last half an hour of a movie that he'd seen already, before drifting off into a light, drunken sleep.

Chapter 3
The day after Boxing Day – three damaged dryers

"Jack Daniels and Coke and a Vodka and Tonic, s'il vous plait."

"Ice in those?" replied the young barmaid.

"Yes please."

"That'll be thirteen pounds."

"Put it on my card will you?" replied Rick. He then turned round to face Tom who was leaning up against the bar next to him.

"So what's with the long face Tomski?" Rick liked to give people nicknames, which changed from month to month. The habit had gone from being slightly endearing, to embarrassing when mentioned in front of other people outside their close circle of friends to being, at this point in time, very annoying.

"I've had a bit of a bad week, as it happens," Tom replied, but even he was taken aback by how insensitive Rick was being, what with his granddad dying and the problem about probably losing his business. Tom had told Rick all about it on the phone that afternoon. Rick asked the question while he was staring at a group of young girls messing around on the dance floor.

Tom had been to Rick's club several times before but never so sober. One of those times had been when he first met Chloe, nearly three years ago. After a lot of Dutch courage, which included a large part of a bottle of champagne and several whiskey and cokes, he went over to her and introduced himself. It was just after he'd opened his first art gallery, so he was feeling confident. It was one of those rare occasions when Tom beat Rick to a girl and managed to hold her attention for the entire evening, without his friend taking over.

It was different tonight but he couldn't quite put his finger on what it was. The layout was how he recalled it, with the dance floor in the middle surrounded by sofas of varying shapes and sizes, comfy chairs and coffee tables, which produced a laid back atmosphere. There were two clear walkways to the left and right of the sofas, and then sofa seats and tables around the walls on each side. The sofa covers were made of a deep sumptuous red velvet material; the tables were dark, mahogany wood. The lighting in the corners and sides was soft and subtle. Spotlights were positioned behind several circular, half-moon tables, the seats to these were moulded into the walls.

Tom eventually worked out that it was the music. Normally around this time of the evening the sounds were a lot more subtle. Not upbeat enough to dance to, but fast enough to get your foot tapping. Teasing you with an electronic beat that could have exploded into a more intense tune, but never quite delivered on what they promised. The DJ would then build on this, progressively raising the tempo until everyone was on their feet.

Tonight had an air of expectation that exceeded normal levels. It was the day after Boxing Day. Only the hardcore London singletons were out enjoying themselves before they started work again in the New Year. After what seemed like a long time, Rick managed to peel his eyes away from the girls on the dance floor to look at Tom, who was still leaning against the bar, pushing down the ice-cubes in his glass of whiskey and coke with his index finger.

"Come on, mate, you're never going to meet someone with a face like that."

"That's the point. I don't want to meet anyone else, I want Chloe back." Rick, who'd only been paying sporadic attention to their conversation up until this point, suddenly became a lot more attentive.

"Back up there my friend. Did I just hear you correctly? You want Chloe back?"

"Yes," said Tom, who felt that by making this admission he was about to open himself up to another lecture from Rick. Although at this stage he was past caring.

"I've done a lot of thinking and I know she ran out on me for some other guy, but I know that, well, I still love her." As he said this, Tom stood up straight, as if he wanted to be counted for something he believed in.

"How much thinking is a lot? Man, you've got to get a grip". Rick also had the rather irritating habit of using 'man' a lot to over-dramatise things.

"Now let me just get the facts straight. She dumped you on Christmas Eve. Kept the Christmas present you bought her of a weekend away in Paris for two, plus the fifteen, I repeat, fifteen big ones you lent her, to help her with her little cash flow problem". When he said this Rick made a quote mark gesture with his index and middle fingers. "You then found out that she'd taken the Paris trip, not with her girlfriend because you bumped into what's-her-name in Blackheath village, but with another man. And you only discovered that because she eventually returned one of the hundred text messages and emails you sent her..."

"It was no more than half a dozen," interrupted Tom, but stopped himself dead in his own tracks when he realised how lame he sounded.

"Yes, ok, whatever, and it wasn't until you turned up unannounced at her flat at eleven o'clock at night, that she finally told you the truth, but wouldn't let you in her flat because...?"

"He was most likely there," Tom quietly admitted.

"That's right Tomski. Her bed was still warm from when you were there and now it was being occupied by her new mystery man. My point is…" and then Rick paused as if he'd lost his way.

"Where is the trust?" said Tom as if he'd heard the speech a thousand times.

"Exactly man, where is the trust?"

"I'm not sure. All I know is that I love her and I'm just not interested in anyone else." Tom took a deep breath and then let out a long and painful sigh.

"So, what do you, propose, to do, about it, exactly," Rick said distracted by a girl as she walked in front of them.

"I don't know, call her up, tell her that what she did doesn't matter. Tell her she can come back."

"Look Tomski, I'm your friend, and I've known you a long time and I would never tell you what to do and it's only my advice…" he said putting his hands on his chest "…but I think you and me should have a few more of these fine beverages and take your mind off this whole 'getting back with your ex-girlfriend' by letting me ask those two lovely ladies over there if they'd like to come and join us for a few light refreshments. What do you say?"

Tom glanced over at the two girls who were wearing short skirts and revealing tops. He slowly turned back to Rick and shrugged his shoulders in submission.

*

"I was with her for three years. Well two years, eleven months and four days. That's got to mean something right? I mean we had something special, really rare, you know, we were, well, we were like perfect for each …"

"Woohoo I love this tune, I love it. Havin' it large," Tamara shouted out as she jumped up from her seat. Her ambition was to be a famous actress after she'd recently got a small part in a teenagers'

TV series. She couldn't have been more than seventeen years old. At first Tom misheard her and reacted by reaching for his jacket pocket, where he was pretty sure he had half a packet of menthol tunes.

"Come on Jodie, let's dance, wicked." She grabbed Jodie's hand and had to wrench her away from Rick's clutches to get her onto the dance floor. Jodie blew Rick a cheeky kiss goodbye and he returned the gesture. He then took the opportunity to slide over, round the half moon seat, to have a word with Tom.

"What are you doing, man?"

"What do you mean, what am I doing. I'm talking, having a conversation, about something a bit deeper than how quickly my car can go from nought to sixty and what a shame it was that S-club 7 ever split up."

"Ha, ha, very funny, you know you really should have thought more about that alternative career as a comedian. No, what I'm talk-ing about is, what's with all the Chloe this and Chloe that and 'Do you think I should call her?' and 'How would you feel if your ex-boyfriend wanted you back even though you went off with another man?' and 'Do you believe, like I do, that there is one soul-mate out there for each of us?' Christ you sound like…"

"Come on, let's hear it, I sound like what?" For the first time since Tom could remember, he was starting to lose his temper.

"You sound so desperate, man. Can't you just lighten up a little and, I don't know, talk about, well anything apart from Chloe?"

"Perhaps I don't want to talk about anything else. Perhaps that's all that's on my mind at the moment. Perhaps you just don't under-stand because, well, you don't know what it's like to miss someone so much that they're all you ever think about, day in and day out, week in and week out. They consume your every thought, your every emotion and every feeling that you have." Tom wanted to say because all you think about is yourself but he knew he'd regret it and he wasn't drunk enough, or angry enough, to want to lash out and hurt his friend's feelings.

"Look, I'm going to the toilet." Tom got out from around the side of the table and made his way across the dance floor, being careful to avoid Jodie and Tamara in case he was forced to join them in their bump and grind session.

Tom would be thirty-five next birthday and he felt like he was entering that stage in his life where he was flattered that a seventeen-year-old would find him attractive, rather than old and a bit past it, and thinking 'You could be my daughter' and 'Should you be out wearing such suggestive clothing?' and 'Have you noticed that we have absolutely nothing in common?' For starters you think that Dexy's Midnight Runners are a nocturnal charity athletics team, that Winston Churchill is a car insurance salesman and that Rap music is really good.

He pushed open the door to the men's room but hesitated before entering. It looked dark and uninviting. Rather than there being a line of cubicles and a set of urinals like most men's toilets, this place had cubicles randomly placed in alcoves and hidden round corners. All passages converged into a central area, where there was a toilet attendant standing in front of a table. On the table was an array of brightly coloured bottles of aftershave and sprays. Sticks of chewing gum and half a dozen boiled sweets were neatly displayed in a silver dish. The attendant insisted on handing out paper towels for people to wipe their hands on before they'd even had a chance to wash them properly. He stood hovering behind them like an over keen sales assistant. Tom checked his trouser pocket for loose change but couldn't find any. He looked around and noticed that there were a few electric hand dryers tucked away. He was in a bad mood and didn't much fancy the idea of giving the attendant a fiver for a stick of gum and a bit of toilet paper, so he decided that after he'd finished in the toilet, he would dry his hands using one of them instead. A cubicle came free and he went in.

After locking the door, he pulled down the lid and placed himself on the toilet. He wanted some time alone, to think. The conclusion he soon reached was that he should phone Chloe tomorrow. Meet up with her and tell her that life was too short for arguments. That they were meant for each other. And, if she didn't mind too much, could he have the £15,000 back, which he'd only intended to give her as a loan. It's just that his business was about to go down the toilet along with the rest of his life, if she didn't help him. Of course because she loves him, even though she's proud and stubborn, she will agree to both. Tom could then put it together with the money his granddad left him. Somehow he would find the other £25,000, save his business and they would live together again; happily ever after.

Tom jumped up and then purposely strode out of the cubicle, enthused by his decision. He went to a sink and began washing his hands, which unfortunately soon turned into a laborious task mainly because he'd made the mistake of using Bar Enema's cheap, sticky soap. He looked up and saw the attendant was being distracted by a talkative customer. He seized his opportunity, went over to one of two electric hand dryers and pressed the button. It didn't work straight away, so he pushed his hands right underneath because sometimes they're a bit insensitive and they don't register unless you do that. Again nothing happened and Tom started to get annoyed. He quickly tried the dryer next to it but got the same inert response.

He looked round and spotted a third electric dryer in an alcove across from where the attendant was standing. He still hadn't noticed Tom as there was a bit of a rush on and he was busy handing out paper towels. Tom tutted to himself and scampered over there with his wet hands. He banged the button and put his hands under the channel for the hot air. It didn't work either and it was at that point he really did lose his temper. He started with a few hard knocks on the side of the machine with the palm of his hand. His actions soon became more aggressive. It was like he wanted to hurt the machine. Punish it for not doing its job properly. For not helping him when he needed it the most. For not being there when things were bad, when his wet and tired hands needed comforting.

"Hey, what are you doing?" shouted the toilet attendant.

Tom didn't bother replying he just kept on bashing the electric hand dryer, to the point where he stood back a little to get some space for a proper kick. Using his right foot for the attack, he kicked so hard that he nearly ripped his trousers. First he did this in a kind of upward motion, like kicking a football, and then he stood back a bit further and karate kicked it with the sole of his foot. It was worth it because the dryer came loose from the wall. He then put his hands around it and wrenched it from the sockets. The occupants of Bar Enema's men's toilet stood and watched with their mouths open as Tom casually dropped it on the ground. He then adjusted his shirt, brushing off any loose bits of plaster before calmly strolling out through the toilet door, into the open space of the club dance floor.

*

Tom didn't actually smash up the electric hand dryer. It was what he wanted to do at the time, but instead he ended up giving the attendant five pounds for a piece of chewing gum, a boiled sweet and a squirt of some cheap cologne he couldn't remember the name of. Espionage or something like that. He then made his way back out to the lovely ladies, Jodie and Tamara, for some more deep and meaningful conversation.

"So what star sign are you?" Tom asked in a half-hearted attempt to make small talk. Rick overheard this and gave him another one of those looks. It was a 'don't mess this one up again' type of look. And so Tom gave him a look back as if to say 'I really don't care what you think'. As it happened, Tom had thought about asking loads of different questions, which included 'What kind of music are you into?' 'Have you ever been abroad?' and 'Did you know that there are fifty different types of nits but 95% of all bites are attributable to only one type and it is the female of the species which is the pain in the neck, so to speak.' The last one, he had to admit, was more a statement than a question. He never got that far.

"Libra."

"Oh, I'm Cancer." There was a brief pause.

"How funny, I thought you were going to say something clever then, like Librans, they're really secretive or passionate, but have a tendency to be too loyal, or can be a bit short tempered, or that Librans are a great match with Cancerians." Tom didn't know what to say, so he smiled.

"What's that smell? Can you smell that Jodie?"

"Na," Jodie replied. She then tilted her head back and proceeded to expand the piece of pink gum she had in her mouth to make a fairly substantial bubble, which eventually burst but was then quite expertly sucked back into the cavern from whence it came.

"Smells like cat wee or something like that," said Tamara.

Tom turned his head so he could subtly smell the shoulder of his shirt, in such a way that he hoped it wouldn't arouse any suspicion. He took a deep breath and realised that he was in fact the source of the feline irritation. It must have been the cologne that he'd sprayed on when he was in the toilets.

"Anyway, I really like your friend," Tamara said turning to her left to talk to Rick, who continued to be all over Jodie like a hot rash. "He's really, well, different." She then turned back to Tom and started rubbing his head, as if he was her pet dog. Tom instinctively pulled away. A move which, in hindsight, probably marked the beginning of the end of a relationship that could have been really beautiful, but was never allowed to blossom. It would appear that Librans and Cancerians aren't a good match after all. Tom's gesture of churlish-ness proved to be the final straw. The one that broke Tamara's will to want to keep trying anymore. To give her some credit, she had made every effort to get on with him even though both people knew there wasn't any chemistry, and that made Tom think. Wasn't it time for her to go home and play with her chemistry set, rather than his hair, it was probably safer.

"What's your problem?" said Tamara who retaliated by pulling away as well.

Tom wanted to say 'well you are, of course.' The trouble was that unlike so many other times in his life when he'd held back from saying what was on his mind, this time he actually said it.

"You're my problem," he replied.

"Really, well I've had enough of this. I take it all back. You're boring; about as much fun as a wet weekend in, in, Bognor." And then she laughed at her own comment. Tom automatically looked over to Rick for a bit of support but without consciously expecting any. Rick started smirking, clearly enjoying the fact that a teenage girl was giving Tom a hard time. Tamara then looked to Jodie for back up and got the appropriate response. Jodie appeared to be a little reluctant at first, but that was mainly because it was such an effort for her to disengage from Rick, who seemed to have more limbs than an octopus.

"Sorry, but I'm going to, have to, leave."

"Come on Jodie, I don't want to spend another moment with this loser," said Tamara, as she put her left hand on her forehead, in an attempt to form the 'L' shape with her thumb and index finger. The full impact, however, wasn't felt because she should have done it with her right hand. Tom was quite surprised, not at the great eloquence of Tamara's exit speech but at the lack of protesting done by Rick who, by this stage of the proceedings had broken into a bout of hysterical laugher.

"I've got to admire your way with the ladies there Tom."

"Thanks, thanks very much for all your help."

"What do you mean, you didn't need my help. You were doing a perfectly good job of messing it up on your own."

"Why are you so happy?" Tom asked. Rick responded by pulling out a piece of paper from the back pocket of his trousers.

"Here, my friend, is the magic number," Rick said waving the piece of paper in the air. It had Jodie's mobile telephone number written on it.

"You won't be so happy when they arrest you for interfering with a minor. Don't worry though, I'll come and visit you in prison."

"Jealousy will get you nowhere."

"Jealous of you, don't delude yourself."

"Come on, plenty more fish in the sea, Casanova. No hard feel-ings. What do you want to drink?" Rick asked, standing up to go to the bar.

"The usual."

On his return, whenever Tom tried to steer the conversation onto his situation with Chloe, Rick would change the subject, which most of the time meant talking about himself. Tom kept on knocking back the drinks until the rest of the evening became a bit of a blur; the night's entertainment culminating in a taxi ride home and Tom then falling into bed in the early hours of the morning.

Chapter 4
28th December – four reasons to meet

Tom was sitting at his dining room table, although he didn't actually have a dining room as such. It was a big open plan lounge, come dining room, come kitchen, with great views of a very cold looking river Thames.

'You owe me another chance' he wrote on a plain piece of A4 paper. Sounds too pushy he thought and put several lines through it.

'We owe it to each other.' "God no, now that sounds too melo-dramatic," he said to himself. 'We owe it to other people?' "No." 'Meet up with me or the hamster gets it.' He screwed up the piece of paper and after a few practice swings, threw the ball across the room. It hit the lip of a small black leather bin and bounced out onto the floor, nestling itself between half a dozen other balls of screwed up paper. His quiet flat was brought to life by the sound of the ringtone on his mobile phone.

"Da...da da dah...da da dah...der der der der derh...da...da da dah...da da dah...der der der der derh..."

He had to move quickly because his phone was also on vibrate and in danger of buzzing itself off his glass topped table.

"Hello."

"When are you going to change that ringtone?" asked Rebecca.

"When you next wash your clothes, probably."

"Shut up. Why do you always have to bring that up?"

"Because it embarrasses you."

"How many times do I have to explain, I'm not the dirty child I used to be."

"Well how do you explain the fact that dad's nickname for you is still grubby pants."

"Tom, do you have to. You know it's because our parents are insensitive and cruel and throughout our lives have tried to make us feel inferior. Anyway, however much I'd like to pursue this interesting subject, I'm in a bit of a hurry so I'll get to the point. Are you still on for ice skating today?"

"Yes, definitely. When have I let you down?"

"Never really, it's just that after what happened to granddad I thought you might not be up for it."

"Yes, no. Thanks for being so considerate, but the show must go on."

"Everything's a song to you, ehh."

"What do you mean? I just feel that at the moment life's a roller-coaster and you've just got to ride it."

"Is that Boyzone?" Rebecca asked, sounding unsure of herself.

"No it was Ronan Keating actually, after…"

"Saddo."

"Oops I did it again."

"No more, I can't take it. Look, is it alright if we meet up at the ice rink at three o'clock?"

"Could you make it four? Only I've got a few things I need to sort out first."

"Yes, ok. See you there."

"Love you."

"You too, bye."

"Bye."

Tom was left sitting at his dining table, staring at his mobile phone. He pressed a few buttons and pulled up Chloe's telephone number. He then finally plucked up the courage and pushed the key pad to dial, with the full expectation that he would be sent straight through to her answer machine.

"Hello."

"Hi it's Tom. Are you ok to talk?"

"Yes, yes I'm fine. Actually I've been meaning to call you. Are you free to meet up with me?"

"Yes ok, I mean no. I mean, yes I'd like to meet up with you," replied Tom, stumbling over his words like a drunk man on a night bus. He then almost fell off his dining room chair in a delayed reaction to the fact that, not only did Chloe pick up the phone, she wanted to meet up with him as well. The only drawback with the unexpectedly smooth running of this conversation was that the speech which he'd spent most of the morning compiling to convince her as to why she should meet up with him became null and void in an instant.

"Is tomorrow ok?" Chloe asked.

"Yes."

"Lunchtime alright?"

"That's fine."

"St. Christopher's Place, that little pancake restaurant on the corner?" Tom couldn't explain it, the extent of his dislike, but he really, really hated pancakes.

"Sounds good."

"Great, well I'll see you at twelve."

"Ok."

"Ok bye then." Tom waited for a reply but all he got was the cold, soulless sound of the dialling tone.

*

"How much is it?" Tom asked the woman in the kiosk.

"£9 for an hour. There are a few spaces for the next session if you want to go off soon."

"Would you mind getting these, it's just I'm a bit short of cash at the moment?" asked Rebecca.

"No, I don't mind," said Tom, although in a small way he did. It certainly increased the odds that his little sister could be the benefactor he was looking for to save his ailing business. To be fair, she was ten years younger than him, so his expectations weren't high to begin with.

"You look terrible, by the way."

"Thanks, I really respect your honesty."

"No I'm serious, for someone who doesn't do that much, you look like you haven't slept properly for weeks."

"No, I'm serious, thanks for sharing your thoughts but next time feel free to keep them to yourself."

"Woooo we're a bit touchy today. Bear's got a sore head. Another night out with that creep Rick in Bar Enema no doubt, ehh Tomo."

"It's Tomski at the moment, actually." Her comment made Tom smile though. "I don't think he's a creep."

"That's because you're a man. He kept trying to grope my bum".

"When did he do that?"

"What do you mean, when? At every opportunity he could."

"So that's why you accidentally knocked that drink over onto his lap," Tom said, sounding like a great mystery had been solved.

"Well someone had to defend my honour and it didn't look like it was going to be you."

"Sorry about that."

"That's alright, I'm a big girl now. I can look after myself."

"I always thought he was a big hit with the girls."

"Yeah, the ones that haven't got two GCSEs to rub together and the main criteria they use to choose their boyfriend is how fast his car goes. Anyway, let's not waste our breath on Mr. 'have you seen my Boxster?' How's Chloe? Has she got over her mystery illness yet?"

Tom immediately picked up on Rebecca's scepticism over Chloe's fake ailment. They walked through and joined the back of the queue to hire ice skating boots.

"Well, like I said they think it's an errh, thyroid problem," Tom said pointing at his throat.

"That's funny because it didn't stop her from going shopping. I bumped into her on Oxford Street, a few weeks ago."

"Are you sure? Size 10 please," he said trying to style it out.

"And for you?" The young girl behind the counter asked Rebecca.

"Its alright, I've got my own," she said holding up her boot bag before resting it back on the floor between her legs. "Yes I'm sure Tom. So are you going to tell me what's going on or am I going to have to torture you?" She then grabbed hold of his wrist and pretended to give him a Chinese burn. Or perhaps she was trying to give him a Chinese burn but didn't know how to do it properly; Tom wasn't sure.

"Arrhhh, I give in. Was she with anyone?"

"Her best friend I think. You know the one with blond hair and the fake tan. Why? You've split up with her haven't you? I knew it."

"What is this? Some sort of women's intuition, kind of a voodoo thing? Come on, let's go and put our boots on."

"It's not voodoo, it's because you're such a terrible liar. You always touch your nose and look away. Not to mention the fact that you looked pretty shifty when mum asked after Chloe on Christmas day."

"What are those, text book responses of someone lying?"

"Pretty much. So come on, what happened?"

"Aha, so you're lying. You never did see Chloe out shopping, did you?"

"Of course I did," she said looking straight at him with her eyes wide open. "Now come on, spill the beans."

"Alright, look if I tell you, you've got to promise not to tell mum and dad."

"Cross my heart," she said making the appropriate gesture.

"Well, she dumped me, on Christmas Eve."

"What, a few days ago?"

"No the one before that."

"Over a year ago? My God, when were you planning on telling everyone, in particular me?"

"Well I was hoping we would get back together."

"So what happened?"

"She found someone else. That's about it really."

"Oh Tom I'm so sorry." Rebecca lent over and gave her brother a hug. He tried to hold back but he was already in such a delicate emotional state, that he couldn't stop the tears from welling up in his eyes. Tom held his sister close, so no one could see that he was upset.

"Don't worry. You know that all my girlfriends fancy you."

"You never told me. You never said that before," he said while pulling away from her slightly. She bent forward to look him in the eyes.

"Well ok, most of them do have boyfriends, but Charlie likes you."

"Thanks, Charlie eats people like me for breakfast, literally. Well, my body weight for breakfast."

"Hey shut up, you. I was trying to be nice." She said this and then gently hit him on the side of his arm.

"I know and I kind of appreciate it." He pulled out a handkerchief and wiped away the last of his tears.

"So did she say why, you know, why she moved on?"

"She said lots of things, but the one that hurt the most was that she said I wasn't fun anymore, that I was always miserable?"

"You never did get over what happened, did you?" After Rebecca said this Tom blew his nose on his handkerchief, making a weird trumpet sound. "It wasn't your fault, you know that. It was an accident, it could have happened to anyone. And anyway, look on the bright side, if it hadn't happened I probably wouldn't be here. So be grateful for what you've got."

"Look let's not talk about it, ok?"

"Ok, if you don't want to that's fine with me." She waited for Tom to get his composure back and then stood up, confidently balancing on her blades.

"I lied, by the way."

"What, about seeing Chloe? How did you…?"

"Don't take it personally, it's just we're biologically better at it than you are. Now come on slow coach, catch me if you can," she said with a worldly expression on her face, before charging out onto the ice.

*

"Come on slow coach."

"Woo hoo, hold on, hold on. I nearly went then."

"That's what happens when you go so slow, the ice freezes to the bottom of your skates," Rebecca shouted.

"Right, you're going to pay for that. Watch your back I'm coming through."

But before Tom could catch her up, in one flowing movement, Rebecca twisted her hips round, turned the direction of her body, began ice skating backwards and waving at him at the same time. It made him feel more than a bit inadequate. It was then that he saw his opportunity and, adopting his best speed skating pose, he tried to go through on the inside of what was a small gap due to the large number of people around.

Needless to say there is nearly always at least one poor soul who thinks they can skate if they try hard enough. It just so happened there was one such person. He looked pretty outlandishly dressed in a bright green, blue and red-striped corduroy jacket, which looked like it had been sewn together by someone unqualified to complete such a task. Underneath that was a brown waistcoat and round his neck he wore an enormously long purple scarf, which looked like it was made out of some very itchy material. He appeared in front of Tom, from out of nowhere and out of control. Tom swerved and collided with a girl. They hit each other hip to hip. He took her clean out and they ended up in a heap on the cold ice. The right leg of

Tom's jeans was completely soaked through, which was exactly what he'd been trying to avoid. Normally when this happens the people involved get up quickly and go their separate ways, but not this time.

"I'm really sorry," Tom said as he sat on the ice, feeling a bit shocked.

"Yes, you came from out of nowhere." He looked up and their eyes met for the first time. As far as Tom was concerned she looked perfect. It was as if her eyes were smiling at him and he couldn't help but smile back.

"It was. Well, I was racing my sister."

"Oh the pretty one. She can skate really well. You should get her to give you some lessons."

"Oh right."

"Come on, I'm only kidding. So she's your sister?" As Tom looked up he noticed Rebecca was circling round them, going backwards again and giving him an 'ok' sign with her hand.

"That's right, I'm here with my sister", he said to subtly indicate the lack of girlfriend anywhere.

"What about you? Who are you here with?" he asked, praying she didn't have a boyfriend.

"My friend Karen, who is over there," she said pointing to a worried looking girl, wearing a matching bright red jumper, scarf and hat, who was clinging onto the barrier around the ice rink. "She hasn't been before."

"Here, let me help you up." Tom quickly got to his feet and held out a hand to pull her up. He was concentrating so hard on balancing—and because she was much lighter than he was expecting—he nearly launched her into the air. It meant she was a little off centre and had to hold onto his arm.

"So, do you come here often?"

"Are you trying to chat me up?"

"No, well, perhaps, maybe, well yes I suppose I am." It was then that he got to see her properly. She had the most amazing dark brown eyes which were wide and alive. Although she sounded

English she didn't look it. Her skin had that tone which, even though it was the middle of winter, still looked tanned. The type that would go really brown in the sun. She had long, flowing dark brown hair, so dark in fact it almost looked black, which came down to the middle of her shoulder blades and she was wearing a pair of earmuffs.

"So what's your name?"

"Tom Kruise with a K," he said in a very formal way.

"Well Tom Kruise with a K, I'm Angela," although she was tempted to say Angela Battle with a B.

"Nice bumping into you," was all he could think of saying.

"Yes, you sure know how to show a gal a good time." But he didn't say anything else. He just stood there, the backs of his legs and arms covered in ice that was starting to melt, in the middle of an ice rink packed with people circling around, staring like a child who was watching their favourite TV programme.

"So look, really it was nice bumping into you to, but I'd better be getting back," Angela said pointing towards her struggling friend.

"No, don't go just yet. Look would you like, if you're not busy, because I know that a lot of people are busy, over Christmas, visiting relatives and whatnot and if you are busy then don't worry but if you're not, would you like to, well, go out with me some time," Tom said with an expression that suggested what he was asking was implausible and could only invoke a negative response.

"But I don't know you. You could do this all the time, bump into women on ice rinks and then ask them out."

"But, but, that's my sister over there. She'll vouch for me," Tom said, frantically beckoning Rebecca over to them.

"See, this is my sister." On cue, Rebecca skated up to them, stopping on a sixpence.

"Hi Rebecca, I'm Angela."

"Hi is he bothering you? Because he can be a bit, you know."

"A bit what" Tom said looking distracted. "Look, Rebecca, I was hoping you could vouch for me."

"Ok, no honestly, I can vouch for him. The prison authorities took the electronic tag off several months ago and well, as far as the family's concerned, the past is in the past. He's paid his debt to society and should be allowed a fair crack of the whip like everyone else."

"I like your jacket by the way," commented Angela.

"Thank you," replied Rebecca. "I love your ear muffs."

"Really, you don't think they're a bit too, pink."

"No, honestly, I've been trying to get a pair like that for ages."

"Well there's this great little shop near, I think it's in Carnaby Street, or is it Bond Street. It's called, oh I just can't think of the name of it."

"Look, I'm not a criminal or, for that matter, a creep. What say you give me your number and I take you out some time."

"Honestly, I really don't give my number out to strangers. I'm not that sort of a girl."

"Well what if I give you my number?" She shook her head and smiled.

"Ok, what if I give you my number?" suggested Rebecca. "And then you can phone me and tell me exactly where you got those ear muffs."

"Yeah, ok. Good idea. And you can tell me where you got that lovely jacket."

Chapter 5
29th December – five minutes late

Tom had negotiated his way out of Bond Street tube station and was using a cut through he knew, down by the side of H&M, to get to St. Christopher's Place. As he was walking, he glanced up at the Christmas decorations, which hung across the narrow street several feet above eye level arranged in a row, getting smaller as they repeated into the distance. Luminescent strip lights and snowflakes were this year's theme.

He loved this particular spot in London: a collection of cafés and restaurants with plenty of chairs and tables outside in a small square, giving it a continental atmosphere. It was busy all the year round, even in the middle of winter. Today, however, he paid his surroundings only fleeting attention. Instead he was more concerned that he wasn't on time. He hated being late even by a few minutes. At the same time he hoped that there weren't any spaces at Café Creperie, so they would have to go some place else.

As he walked round the corner, he spotted Chloe sitting amongst a crowd of people with a small make-up mirror in her left hand, applying lipstick with the other. Much to Tom's annoyance, even though it was busy, Chloe had secured a table for two.

"Hi, sorry I'm a bit late."

"Yes, well, I couldn't wait any longer. I've already got myself a drink." Despite not seeing him for nearly a year, Chloe displayed an irritating familiarity in the way she addressed him. She instantly made him feel guilty. After keeping Tom waiting, she eventually put her make-up away, stood up and reluctantly reached her arm round his shoulder, giving Tom a pat on the back.

"Good to see you," Tom said, holding onto Chloe for as long and as tightly as she would allow. She soon broke away though and they settled into their seats.

"Is that a green jumper you're wearing?" They were outside, under one of those mushroom shaped garden heaters. Tom had caught a blast of it on his face and had unbuttoned his coat.

"Yes it is, do you like it?" he asked enthusiastically.

"I thought you hated green?"

"When did I say that?"

"When we were together."

"No, no, I don't remember that. Don't you like it?"

"Look it's not important," she said as if the words were an unwanted piece of chewing gum that she was discarding from her mouth. This wasn't the response that Tom had been hoping for. It was the first prick which, although it didn't exactly burst his 'bubble of hope,' was in serious danger of deflating it.

"Well I'll make sure I don't wear it next time." There was an uncomfortable pause as Tom waited for some reassurance that there would be a next time. Instead Chloe changed the subject.

"So, how are your parents?" she said, pulling out a packet of cigarettes from her handbag, lighting one up and blowing the smoke in Tom's direction. Some got caught in the back of his throat and it made it difficult for him to speak properly.

"They aren't that great really to be honest. Granddad died on

Boxing Day."

"Oh I'm sorry to hear that," she said taking another drag on her cigarette and blowing the smoke in his face again. Tom waited for a follow-up question, but instead she changed the subject again.

"What about your lovely little sister? Meet up for your usual ice skating day, did you?" Tom recalled that the time he spent with his little sister was a bone of contention when they were together, one of many.

"She's good thanks, got herself a new job. Look there was something important I wanted to say, it's the reason I asked to meet up with you."

"You didn't ask to meet up with me, I asked you." Chloe's abrupt tone of voice pushed Tom onto the back foot.

"Ok, well, I phoned you up. Anyway I was wondering if, it's just that I've been doing a lot of…"

"You ok there," asked the waitress.

"No, can I have another latté and a water?" replied Chloe.

"Still or sparkling?"

"Still, and Tom, are you still drinking cappuccinos?" Tom nodded obediently, even though he wasn't that keen on them anymore.

"A cappuccino and, no rush, but could we get the bill as well." Tom had too much on his mind to notice that Chloe was already hatching her escape plan. Then, as Tom began to talk about a subject he'd been meaning to discuss with Chloe since the day she left, the thing that had given him endless sleepless nights, she started to talk over him.

"I have something I need to say…," Chloe said trying to look as humble as she could.

"I know we've had our differences, but at the end of the day…' Tom said, as he began to spill his heart out, initially oblivious to Chloe's interruption.

"…I've got engaged."

"…you're what?"

"You know, with the view to getting married." He heard a loud popping noise in his head. When he looked at her, he could see she was struggling not to break into a smile. Chloe was one of those girls who'd been planning her wedding day since her seventh birthday. Tom lost the use of his voice. His jaw kept moving but nothing was coming out. Music from the pub across the road came wafting through the air, getting louder as Tom began to focus on it. He soon recognised the record; it was 'Last Christmas' by Wham.

*

"I just don't understand why you can't be happy for me," Chloe said, taking one long final drag from her cigarette before stubbing it out.

"Don't know why you can't tell me who you're marrying?" It was turning into a deadlock that neither appeared to be prepared to break. Tom was imagining he'd crashed Chloe's wedding and, after shoving the groom's head in the wedding cake, he began to strangle the said low-life until he'd gone blue. The only trouble was, the face he kept on visualising for some bizarre reason was his old Maths teacher, Mr. Jones.

"You can act like such a little boy sometimes, do you know that? I'm getting married and it's not to you, so just deal with it."

This was Chloe's answer to everything, 'Just deal with it'. You're not happy, so 'deal with it'. Oh really, you were involved in a tragic accident when you were young? 'Deal with it'. Your parents have blamed you the rest of your life for what happened? 'Deal with it'.

"Is that it then, you're getting married, life's great for you. Everything about us is now a distant memory. If someone asks you if you ever knew someone called Tom, you'd say I vaguely remember the name but no, I can't picture the face."

"You think it's been so easy for me, don't you?" she said leaning forward, pressing her right index finger hard on the table, to emphasise her anger. "Well let me just say that breaking up with you, having to hear your incessant demands for me to come back all the time, wasn't easy. Coping with the break-up and holding down my job, wasn't easy. Listening to you whining on the phone at me every five minutes, asking me where it all went wrong. That wasn't easy either, especially while I was trying to build a new relationship, I can tell you."

Tom hadn't seen this bombshell coming and his emotions were all over the place. It shook him to the very core and he was experiencing that awful feeling of anxiety you get when something terrible and unexpected happens. It made him want to hide away. Lock himself in his flat, pull all the curtains and order take-aways for the rest of the month. It was as if his heart was a flower bed and, after abandoning it and letting the weeds grow, Chloe had just trampled all over it.

"It wasn't like I had the sort of income at my disposal that you had either, you know, an estate agent's wages aren't that great."

"What about the fifteen thousand…" Tom lowered his voice and lent forward in his metal seat, "…what about the money I lent you, that must have softened the blow a bit."

"What are you talking about?" Chloe said looking dismissively at Tom. "You never lent me that money. You gave it to me."

"No, I told you at the time it was a loan."

"How very conditional of you. Whatever happened to the Tom I used to know, the one who would do anything for me? Remember when you said our love transcended all earthly possessions".

"Yes, well, that was before you swapped me and my earthly possessions for someone else. Come on Chloe don't be unreasonable, I need that money back."

"I haven't got any money and what little I have I'm spending on the wedding."

"So you're spending my money on your wedding. That's great, isn't it. How appropriate."

"No, no, I had loans to pay off and stuff," she said unable to look Tom straight in the eye.

"What sort of stuff?"

"Look I can't help you, I haven't got your damn money, ok? I only

wanted to meet up with you to tell you I was getting married, so you
didn't hear it from someone else."

"Well how very gracious of you."

"Tom, if you're going to be like that."

"Like what?"

"Come on Tom where's your Christmas spirit?"

"You spent it."

This led to another stalemate. They sat across from each other,
their bodies turned away slightly, with their arms and legs crossed.
When the waitress came over with the bill, on a small silver dish, she
quickly sensed the tense atmosphere, diplomatically laid it between
them in the middle of the table, turned on her heels and walked off.
Tom glanced down at it and then pushed it in Chloe's direction.

"I can't pay for it, I didn't bring enough money with me," she said
glaring at Tom.

"What about using the credit card that I so generously paid off
then?"

"I forgot my credit card," she said hanging her head. Then the
waterworks started. "I don't understand why you hate me so much."

"Look I don't hate you." And just like that, as if he were a badly
mixed soufflé, Tom crumbled in an instant.

"Yes you do."

"No I don't."

"You look at me like you hate me."

"It's ok, I'll get this one." Then, as if Tom had ushered the magic
words, she stopped crying: like she was a tap and Tom had turned
her off.

"Thanks Tom, I really appreciate that," she said looking away and
rubbing her nose.

*

"I know I've paid the bill but is it possible for me to get a hot
chocolate and could you clear this away for me please?" Tom said

to the waitress, pointing at the untouched cappuccino. Chloe was long gone, making some excuse that she had to pop in and feed her next door neighbour's cat. Given that she probably didn't know her neighbours and she hated cats, her excuse seemed more than a little implausible. Tom was left sitting on his own in the crowded restaurant, full of animated people in a place that he didn't even like that much.

What a mess, he thought. What a complete joke his life had turned out to be. It was at moments like this he could understand why some people didn't want to be here anymore. Why didn't she love him? Why doesn't anyone love him for that matter?

The reality of his situation was starting to sink in. Chloe was getting married. Why couldn't he let her go? They say that if you really love someone then you should let them go. What was that all about? What, you let them go so you spend the rest of your life wishing it away because you miss them so much? No, it should be if you love someone then you tie them in, trap them in your world and then make them realise they can't live without you.

It started to snow. Not a heavy fall, just the odd flake nonchalantly meandering its way down from the heavens. A few snowflakes landed on Tom's table, distracting him from his predicament. He held out his hand as some more glided towards him. As soon as he tried to capture one, it melted. The symbolism of the event was lost on him though. Core to everything was that he missed his granddad and, more than at any other time in his life, he could do with his advice.

"Do you mind if I sit here? It's just that it's so busy at the moment," asked the grey haired man. He was in his late fifties and had an amicable smile.

"No not at all."

"Doesn't seem cold enough to snow," he continued.

"I think it might be these heaters," Tom said pointing to the one closest to him.

"Yes, how silly of me. Arthur's the name."

"Hi I'm Tom Kruise with a K," Tom replied leaning across the table to shake hands. Arthur had a book in his left hand which he placed on the table.

"Good book?" Tom asked in an attempt to make polite conversation.

"Yes, yes it is."

"What's it about?"

"Well in a nutshell, without giving too much away, just in case you wanted to read it, it's about a man who always puts his energy into the wrong relationships. His girlfriend takes advantage of his good nature and uses him for what she can before she moves onto someone else. His friends never tell him the truth and laugh about him when his back's turned."

"Sounds like he's a bit of a loser this guy."

"Actually I think the opposite, but travelling along life's highway, so to speak, he's lost his way. Something terrible happened to him when he was young and he's let it affect the rest of his life."

"So what happens to him, this lost soul?"

"Like so many people, it's only when he hits rock bottom that he wises up. It's only when things can't get any worse that he decides to do something about it. He changes from within and then he begins to realise that there are people around him that do care about him. It's just that he was putting all his energy into the ones who kept taking from him. He…"

Arthur was interrupted by the sound of a vehicle screeching round the corner. It drove down James Street at top speed. Tom lifted himself up out of his seat and managed to catch a glimpse of a blue van as it sped down to the lights at the bottom. It skidded again and then sounded like it had made it through onto Oxford Street.

"Looks like they're in a bit of a hurry," said Tom.

"More haste, less speed, my granddad always used to say," Arthur replied smiling.

"Yes mine too," Tom replied thoughtfully.

Chapter 6
30th December – six sayings you won't forget

Tom had written over half of what he wanted to say. It had been hard, in fact one of the hardest things he'd had to do in a while. How do you sum up a person's life in a few sentences? Sum up what they meant to you and convey that to an audience. He was struggling to tie it all up and was in need of some inspiration, so he flicked on the TV and his PlayStation, loaded up the 80s karaoke disc and then sat down on the sofa with the control.

"Right there's only one thing for it." He clicked a few buttons and then picked up the microphone. "The video began, the music started up and then so did Tom.

"I'm going to take a little time, a little time to think things over." He positioned himself in front of the mirror in the lounge, adopting his best Tony Hadley type pose. Tom was tone deaf. He'd never scored more than 2,000 points out of a possible 10,000 on the easiest setting of his Sing Star.

"I better read between the lines in case I need it when I'm older."

Often, when things got really bad and they were desperate, the neighbours from the flat below would resort to banging on the ceiling with their broom.

"Whooaawooowooooo," he yelled at the top of his voice. Tom became animated, he closed his eyes and pulled his head back to face skywards. His head then fell forward before he dramatically came back up for air, in preparation for the main part of the song.

"In my life there's been heartache and pain. I don't know if I can face it again. Can't stop now, I've travelled so far to change this lonely life. I wanna know what love is …"

"Da…da da dah…da da dah…der der der der derh…da…da da dah…da da dah…der der der der derh…", came the sound of his mobile phone, barely audible above his screeching.

"Bugger," he said as he chucked the microphone on the sofa in annoyance and had to run around to find his phone.

"Hi."

"Tom its Raymond and Robert, we're on a conference call." The time was exactly nine o'clock in the morning.

"Hold on one second," Tom said fumbling for the volume bottom on the remote control. "Is it that time already?"

"The world of finance doesn't wait," replied Robert.

"So did you manage to come up with the money?" asked Raymond.

"No, surprisingly enough the fifty grand we need didn't fall off the money tree which I planted in the back garden."

"There's no need for sarcasm."

"There's no need to close down a perfectly good business."

"Look we've been through this before. Kruise Galleries is hemorrhaging money at the moment, something needs to be done," explained Raymond.

"I've managed to get some of the money,"

"How much of the money?"

"Ten thousand." There was a pause.

"Well it could buy you some time."

"Don't you mean it could buy us some time," Tom pointed out.

"Yes of course," replied Raymond.

"How much time?"

"A couple of weeks."

"Are you kidding me? Ten thousand pounds only buys us a few weeks," Tom replied in disbelief.

"Well let me see" explained Robert, "the interest payments on the loans are almost a thousand pounds a month and the rent on the three galleries is five thousand plus, not to mention staff and overheads, so perhaps I'm exaggerating. It should buy six weeks. Two months at best".

"That's still not great."

"When can you get the money to us?"

"Soon, a few days," Tom replied sounding uncertain.

"Well it's the 30th today. I could keep the wolves at bay until, say, the end of next week. Is that ok?"

"Yeah, yeah that should be ok," Tom said still sounding unsure that it was what he really wanted to do.

"How will you send the money?"

"How do you want the money?"

"Well, to speed things up you could put it into my personal account. That way I can get them to process it that day, especially if you make the transfer on-line."

"Why not put it into the company bank account?"

"You could do that if you want, I was just hoping to get it sorted out a bit quicker and save us a few bob in interest."

"Right, well I'll do that then."

"Anything else?"

"Yes Robert, have you got the breakdown of those sales and cost figures, the ones I asked you for a few weeks ago?"

"Tom, I've explained to you that you're not my only client and anyway, I'm on holiday now."

"Ok well when can you get them to me?"

"I'm out of the office until the 8th, so sometime after that."

"Right that will have to do."

"Good, we live to fight another day. That's got to be a good New Year's omen."

"Yes I guess it must be," replied Tom unable to force a smile.

*

The cars had arrived promptly at one o'clock to take them in a procession to the cemetery. One of Albert's requests was to be buried in Blackheath, next to his wife. Tom had arrived in a car with his sister, two of his cousins and his aunt and uncle on his dad's side.

Albert had been very specific about his wishes. After his wife had died, he realised the importance of leaving a will. In fact, in a macabre way Albert and Tom had jokingly planned it all out. For whatever reason it had never occurred to Tom that it might actually happen. So there they all were, sitting in the main room listening to 'Bohemian Rhapsody' by Queen, which, while also being a favourite of Tom's, was nevertheless one of the longest songs ever recorded. Even from the grave Tom felt that his granddad was pulling everyone's leg. On his coffin was an array of flowers. The largest single piece was a detailed display of a shirt made of hundreds of tiny flowers, with Greavsie written on the back.

"...and now," said the reverend, "Albert's grandson Tom would like to come up and say a few words."

It was only a small audience made up of close relatives and friends. Tom wasn't so much nervous as emotional, trying to hold back any tears. It was quiet as he made his way to the front, apart from the rustle of a coat and the odd cough.

"Errhum," he said clearing his throat. He placed a piece of paper on the wooden podium in front of him and then glanced down at his notes. Before starting to talk into the microphone, he looked up and quickly focused on the congregation.

"Albert always liked to use expressions to sum up a situation. They were a part of his personality. They weren't always appropriate but what I'd give to hear him utter just one of them again."

"Often it's not until loved ones leave us that we reflect on the impact they had on our lives and how they played a large part in making us the people we are today. My granddad played just such a part in influencing me. Anyone who has ever met him knows that he was a larger-than-life character. He made you feel special when you were with him because of the attention he gave you, the way he'd listen to every word that you said. By the time you'd finished talking with him, he knew what you'd been up to for the last ten years, where you wanted it to go over the next ten, and what your view was on anything and everything from music to religion and politics, to the very essence of what makes you the way you are. He'd ask the questions that most people would avoid, but in such a way that you felt respected. Often, it wasn't until afterwards that you'd realised how much you'd opened up to him."

"What he did, he did with passion and with an enthusiasm that was as infectious as his laugh or his smile. His playfulness would drive us all mad but we loved him for it. There isn't one person amongst us who hasn't been shown how to tango properly, who hasn't got drunk on his sloe gin, who hasn't listened to his vinyl record collection or his masterful playing of the banjo." When Tom said this there was a ripple of verbal agreement and a lot of nodding of heads.

"He never inspired me to want to play the banjo, don't get me wrong, but I did want to be as charming and as interesting and as light-hearted as he was. What he did inspire me to do was to set up my own business, to see the world and to play football the way it should be played. Most of all his influence made me want to be honest, open-hearted, thoughtful and, and..."

At this point Tom began to struggle. After doing so well, what he'd said had stirred up his emotions and his words began to get caught in his throat, like a fly in a spider's web. The more he tried to speak, to get them to wriggle free, the more entangled they became.

"I, I, I wanted to, to finish by..." Tom put his hand in his pocket, pulled out a white handkerchief and blew on it. The noise caused feedback in the microphone that was so loud, most people in the front row reacted by wincing or putting their hands over their ears.

"Sorry. I just wanted to finish off by saying, well, like I mentioned if there was one thing my granddad always liked it was a good saying. So here are my six favourite sayings that will always remind me of him."

"Be true to yourself," Tom said slowly, pausing between each one. "As you sow, so you reap. Do as you would be done by. That's as useful as a handbrake on a canoe. And my favourite: when you assume it makes an ass out of you and me." There was a ripple of laughter, almost of relief, as the emotional intensity of Tom's speech had built up over the last five minutes.

"And finally: You can't always get what you want, but if you try sometimes, you might find you'll get what you need." Tom then turned to the reverend, who nodded and went over to a small CD player sat on the floor to the right of Albert's coffin. The room was filled with the sound of choir voices and then the distinctive vocals of Mick Jagger.

Tom slowly made his way back to his seat, in between Rebecca and his cousin, Luke. His sister grabbed hold of his hand and gave it a squeeze. Tom had held it together up until this point but as soon as they looked at each other, the tears began to roll down his cheeks.

*

"So how are you?" Tom asked, while carefully placing two vol-au-vents next to the numerous sausage rolls he'd already built up on his paper plate, which was starting to bend under the strain.

"I'm alright as it goes. Oh yeah, I almost forgot to tell you, I'm thinking of moving to Blackheath. Well, touch wood," Luke said leaning forward and gently tapping his hand on the table. "I've got to sell my place first but there've been a few people who've looked round who are interested."

"Really? So you're coming to my neck of the woods."

"Of course, I forgot you're in Greenwich. Are you still down by the river, along from the Cutty Sark?"

"That's right, just down the road actually, or the hill more like. Granddad used to live in Blackheath before he moved to Westerham," Tom pointed out.

"That's one of the main reasons really. We used to visit Albert there every now and again and I always liked it."

"I'll grab some estate agent stuff for you the next time I'm in the village, if you want?"

"That would be great. If it's not too much trouble?"

"No, no trouble at all."

There was a slightly awkward silence as they started eating the buffet food. The peripheral chat had been exhausted quickly and neither was quite sure whether or not to move onto more personal subjects.

"Albert was a great bloke," Luke said, forcing a smile.

"The best," replied Tom, looking down at his feet.

"I remember his expressions. That was a good speech, I liked that."

"Thanks."

"Once, I'll never forget it, we were all going to the West End to see a musical and we were running a bit late. My mum said we should jump in a taxi and Albert said it would be quicker to walk. Anyway we ended up getting in a cab and almost straight away got caught in traffic. They started arguing and mum said something like 'I assumed that this was the quickest way', and Albert said…"

"When you assume, it makes an ass out of you and me," filled in Tom.

"Exactly, she was so angry, she went as red as this," Luke said pointing to a mini tomato that was on his plate. "Before that I couldn't remember the last time I heard my mum swear. It sounded weird, it was almost like it had been so long she'd forgotten how to do it properly."

"I bet Albert didn't leave it there," commented Tom.

"No you're right he didn't. I think he told her to chill out or some-thing along those lines. It was like adding fuel to the flames if you know what I mean. In fact he came out with another saying which made me laugh, but I can't remember what it was."

"Was it, 'you're as useful as an ashtray on a motorbike'?" Tom said trying to be helpful.

"No but that's a good guess. It was something like that."

"As useful as a one legged man in an arse kicking contest?"

"Yes," Luke said laughing, "that was it. God that was funny."

"He was funny, if not a little bit embarrassing sometimes," said Tom. "I remember when I was fifteen and you know how self-conscious you can be at that age, especially around girls. I went to the school roller-disco, which looking back on it was embarrassing enough in itself. Anyway, he dropped me off at the gates and there was this big group of girls, probably at least ten, which back then was one of the most intimidating things, and in front of all of them, as I was about to shut the car door, he shouted and I mean shouted at the top of his voice, 'see you Tom, be lucky.'"

"Tough break," Luke said smiling.

"You can imagine it can't you; it was a catch phrase which haunted me for the rest of my time at school."

"I know what you mean," sympathised Luke. "He was a real char-acter, wasn't he?"

"I just don't think they make them like that anymore. He was part of that post-war generation, where they always made the best of what they had. Never let anything go to waste," explained Luke.

"Yeah, and the rest. The number of times we'd be eating and he'd ask me if I wanted my last carrot or roast potato. If I said no, and he was full up, he would still put it in a plastic container and eat it the next day."

Tom paused for a second to collect his thoughts. "And he'd say the things to my parents that I'd wanted to say but never had the bottle, especially to my mum. He'd stick up for me and if she was be-ing unreasonable, he'd be able to embarrass her about things she did when she first started going out with dad. Like the time she set fire to the meatloaf."

"It was like he was on our side," said Luke.

"Exactly. The more I think about it, the more I believe that he was the best granddad you could wish for. Don't get me wrong, he wasn't perfect. He played loads of tricks on me and they weren't always funny and he had his quirky little ways. His expressions weren't always appropriate. But his heart was in the right place."

"And he may not have been the best cook in the world but he never forgot you liked your omelette with ham and cheese, or that you liked watching horror movies or episodes of Only Fools and Horses. He never forgot you and what made you the person you are," added Luke. "He'll be missed, that's for sure."

"Yes, he most definitely will," agreed Tom.

"Another vol-au-vent?"

"Why not, he would have liked the food."

"One thing's for sure, he wouldn't have wanted us to waste anything," commented Luke.

"That's true, we mustn't let him down."

Part Two
Dennis Malcolm Leslie Johnston

Chapter 1
Christmas Day – one oversized microwave

"Hello sis. Take those for me would you," Den said in a gruff cockney accent as he handed Sharon a couple of bottles of red wine, while kissing her on the cheek.

"Thought you was on the wagon?"

"That's right, that's why I don't need them any more," explained Den. Michael, Sharon's eldest, appeared from round the side of his mum, holding a large, purple, angry looking plastic robot in his hand. He watched Den intently as he went back to his van, opened the boot and had a brief struggle trying to pull out a large pile of presents. Sharon followed him and then helped him slam the boot. When Den was close enough Michael aimed the disk, which was in the robot's chest, pressed a button and watched as it flew through the air and hit Den on the forehead, right between his eyes.

"Michael, how many times have I told you? Don't fire that thing at people, least of all your Uncle."

"That's alright" said Den. "Hello Mickey, Happy Christmas." Michael didn't reply, instead he ran out and grabbed the plastic disk, which was lying on the grass.

"Look what Uncle Den's brought you," said Sharon while simultaneously placing her hand over the belly of Michael's robot.

"Where's Ron?"

"Where do you think?" Sharon said putting a cigarette in her mouth.

"Entertaining Kylie and Kim with some new magic tricks, while he takes a much needed break from putting the finishing touches to the newly redecorated lounge?"

"Very droll bruv; mind that step, we don't want you having an accident now, do we," she said with a sarcastic expression on her face. Den made his way down the narrow hallway of his sister's four bedroom council house in Greenwich. On opening the door to the lounge he saw his brother-in-law, sitting on their bright, floral red and white sofa. Den could have sworn he was in the same position he left him in over a week ago, surrounded by a similar number of empty beer cans.

"Alright Denny." Ron greeted Den without diverting his gaze away from the enormous flat screen TV, which almost filled the whole of the end wall.

"Not bad, not bad at all. Merry Christmas."

"Same to you."

"Where can I put these?" Ron gestured with his beer can towards a short plastic Christmas tree; crammed in the corner of the room to make way for the huge TV.

"Help yourself to beers, they're in the fridge."

"Do you want one?" asked Den, feeling that there was no point explaining to his brother-in-law that he wasn't drinking alcohol anymore. Ron took a long hard look at the can that was nestled snugly in the palm of his hand, resting on his not insubstantial beer belly. He lifted it up slightly to assess the weight of its contents.

"Yeah, why not, it's Christmas after all." As Den entered the kitchen he was greeted with the usual scene of anarchy.

"Michael. Michael. Get your hand out of the toaster. How many times have I told you not to do that? Kylie. Kylie, stop." Sharon ran over to her five-year-old daughter, grabbed hold of the back of her T-shirt and then pulled her out of the kitchen bin. It was a different world when compared to the serenity of the front living room.

"Ron wants another beer."

"Oh he does, does he. Well tell Ron that I don't want him spoiling his appetite for a dinner that I've spent the last four hours slaving over."

"I've got a better idea," suggested Den. "Why don't you tell him yourself?"

"Thanks bruv."

"Quite alright. Look, why don't we take a few minutes out and go and open the presents I bought. I got you something special."

"Is it electricule?"

"Maybe."

"Can I cook stuff in it?"

"Maybe."

"You didn't, did you?" Sharon said, her voice migrating into a high pitched shriek. She pulled off her oven gloves and shouted at the top of her voice,

"Michael, Kylie, Kimmy. Living-room. Now. Uncle Den's got some presents for you." Like a mini cyclone with its epicentre on the move, Sharon's children changed course from the kitchen to the lounge leaving a trial of destruction in their path. On entering the room, Sharon marched over to the TV, reached behind and switched it off at the plug.

"Hang on, I was watching..." Ron started saying, but on catching the expression on his wife's face, chose the wiser of two options.

"Ok, what have we got here then," Sharon said grabbing hold of the top present.

"Kylie, this one's for you." Sharon's eldest daughter trotted up dutifully and took the present from her mum. "Michael..." but before she could finish her words, without taking more than a few small paces, he'd jumped like a professional basketball player and snatched the present from his mother's grasp. "And last but by no means least, little Kimmy."

There was a brief moment while paper was ferociously torn apart, Sharon's children acting like a pack of hungry hyenas feeding on their Christmas present prey. Michael was the worst, almost sending his present into orbit as he pulled at it viciously, tearing off lumps of wrapping paper to quickly expose what was inside. They didn't look quite so enthusiastic when each of them discovered what their present was: a box of assorted chocolates.

"So this large one left must be for mummy. I wonder what it could be." Sharon said in an annoyingly childish voice. In a display of savagery, equal to the one shown by her children a few moments earlier, she disposed of the silver and white snowflake wrapping paper in a matter of seconds.

"A microwave. Ron, look what Den's bought us."

"Top of the range, that. State of the art technology," commented Den.

"Does look quite big, Den," commented Sharon.

"Well, have you seen the size of your husband," Den said laughing.

"Oi less of that," smiled Ron, "I'll have you know I'm starting my new fitness regime in the New Year."

"What's that? Shaz, will you be hiding the remote control from now on?"

"Ha, ha, very funny," Ron said, but as he shifted his weight on the sofa, one of the legs gave way and he was jolted downwards, spilling the contents of his can of beer down the front of his white T-shirt.

*

"Den, would you mind setting up the microwave for me so I can cook the Christmas pud?" Sharon asked, slurring her words a little from the red wine.

"I'll tell you what, I'll cook it for you if you want. How long do they take?"

"Don't know. It should say on the back of the packet. Only a few minutes I reckon. Your present is fantastic Den. Normally it would take me hours to cook the thing."

"That was a beautiful meal by the…" Den was interrupted by Ron who let out the most enormous burp. This was then followed by a mini-burp from Michael.

"Ron, do you mind? We got company."

"Come on darlin'. That's a sign of appreciation in some countries."

"Well we ain't anywhere else. We're in south London so shut your gob."

Den felt that this would be a good time to head off to the kitchen, where he found Sharon and Ron's Christmas present perched precariously on the sideboard. It looked enormous in their tiny kitchen. Den prised open the cardboard box and spent a few minutes searching for the instruction manual but when he found one, it was all in Japanese.

"Can't be that difficult," he said to himself as he pulled off all the plastic and foam wrapping which had held it in place. It came with a plug, so he just had to carefully slot it into an already overloaded set of sockets. Den then grabbed hold of the Christmas pudding and turned it upside down.

"Microwave in five minutes," he said reading the instructions out loud. He carefully took the pudding out of its packet and placed it in the middle of the dish inside. The microwave was so large, and from the angle he was staring into it, the pudding looked like a tiny, domed boat floating in the middle of a huge glass ocean. He pushed the door shut and pressed one of the three black buttons on the front. The light came on and the machine started to make a loud whirring noise. He quickly pressed the same button again when he remembered he hadn't set the timer. Up until this stage he'd been relatively calm. When nothing happened, Den felt his first pang of concern in the form of a knot that was forming in the pit of his stomach. He hit the same button several more times and then tried pushing the button next to the one that had started it up. In the meantime the kids, who'd been relatively quiet the last half hour, had been allowed to get down from the dinner table and were tearing around the house.

"Are you alright in there bruv?" Sharon called out from the lounge.

"You haven't blown yourself up have you Den?" Ron said laughing.

"Not yet," Den replied scratching his head. He began to feel an intense heat emanating from the microwave. The whirring sound was getting so loud, it was beginning to drown out the noise being made by the children.

"What's that racket?" Sharon asked poking her head round the kitchen door. When she fully entered the room Den could see she had Michael in a headlock under her arm. She soon released him after a quick pat on the head.

"Nothing," replied Den, who'd been reduced to randomly pressing all the buttons on the front of the microwave but soon stopped doing this because they'd become so hot they were starting to burn his fingertips.

"Bruv, I'm no electricule expert but I don't think it's supposed to be making that noise," she shouted.

"I think you could be right," Den shouted back, the sound of his voice almost inaudible by this stage. He slowly began to back away from the microwave, which was now starting to vibrate a bit like a washing machine on a very low spin. He kept going until he reached Michael and Sharon by the door.

"Den you should see the expression on your face: it's a pic…" But before Sharon could finish her sentence there was an almighty bang, like a shotgun being fired. The door of the microwave flew open and its contents were sprayed through the air at Sharon, Michael and Den. Within an instant they were covered from head to toe in lukewarm Christmas pudding. Den grabbed a lump that had landed on his forehead and, after smelling it, licked some off the palm of his hand. It wasn't even cooked properly.

*

"It's engaged again. Come on, hang up the phone will you," Den said impatiently.

"You know what people are like over Christmas, Den. They like to talk to their relatives."

"What am I going do?" Den said looking anxiously at his sister.

"Well where do they live?"

"Charlton Road, not that far from here."

"I reckon you should hop in the van. You'll be round there in a jiffy. Chances are it's sitting in the corner of their living room not being used while Keith's missus is on the phone to someone."

"Knowing my luck..."

"Shut up and get going. The sooner you go, the sooner you can come back and watch Ron fall asleep in front of the telly."

"I heard that," Ron shouted from the living room. "Least I didn't blow up the dessert."

"That's because you don't do nothing Ron. You can't muck it up if you don't do it."

"Ok, good idea sis, thanks," said Den pulling out what he hoped was the last piece of moist Christmas pudding from his hair.

Den arrived at Keith's house in no time at all but the nervous feeling in the bottom of his stomach only got worse when nobody answered the doorbell. He tried peering in through the front window. Unfortunately, the lights were out and the curtains shut.

Part of him thought that everything would be alright, afterall Keith may not have used it. Den could always lie and say the others he'd sold were fine and Keith must have been really unlucky. But there was another part of him, the sober side, which was telling him to follow this through and take responsibility for his mistake.

He had a look round the side of the house and noticed that the gate was slightly ajar. On pushing it open, he immediately saw signs of life: light from a kitchen window, the faint sounds of Christmas music and muffled voices. If he held onto the ledge and stood on the tips of his toes, he found he could just see in through the kitchen window.

"Oh no," he said softly when he saw Keith's wife, Cathy, putting a Christmas pudding into her brand new, extremely oversized micro-wave oven. Den took a large gulp of air but refrained from shouting out. Perhaps she'd be fine, he thought, it's not like they're all defi-nitely going to be faulty. But then the by now familiar whirring noise started up which, like the high pitched howling of a fox in the middle of the night, is hard to ignore. Cathy had a bemused expression on her face. She put down her oven gloves and disappeared from Den's line of vision. Within a matter of seconds she reappeared with Keith in tow. Neither of them noticed the top of Den's head peaking over the washing up in the sink. All their attention was on their brand new Christmas present. Den could see Keith's mind working overtime and his first action was to reach for the plug.

"Great idea, why didn't I think of that?" Den said to himself. As a result, Den relaxed and gave himself the luxury of a few moments break from standing so awkwardly on his toes. The trouble was the whirring noise didn't go away. He sprang back up and as he did, he could feel a lump in his jacket pocket. He reached inside and found his mobile phone. A quick search produced Keith's number in a mat-ter of seconds but before he had a chance to dial there was a loud bang and then silence. Den put his mobile phone back in his jacket pocket and then slowly raised himself up to look at what had hap-pened. He was genuinely surprised at how much mess one Christ-mas pudding could make.

Chapter 2
Boxing Day – two disastrous goals

Spurs always lose to Arsenal, thought Den as he weighed up his options. Safe as houses that bet. It could be a draw, local derbies are competitive, but having said that the odds are better putting money on Arsenal to win when they're playing away. He reached inside the back pocket of his jeans, pulled out five ten pound notes and strolled up to the counter.

"Right, I'll have fifty big ones on Arsenal to beat Spurs, my good man."

"No problem," said the man behind the counter. As he was staring at his ticket, Den was broken out of his daydream by another much more pressing thought. He glanced at his watch. It was half past one, so he was already half an hour late to pick up the kids from his ex-wife. He couldn't quite muster a run, so he walked quickly to his van that was parked in a bay on the road.

When Den eventually arrived at Yvonne's council flat, he could see her outside her front door, standing on the top floor walkway of the six storey building. He couldn't be sure from such a distance but it looked like she was clutching a rolling pin, which he imagined she was briskly slapping into the palm of her left hand. He parked and ran into the lift. The rancid odour, which unexpectedly hit him in the face, made him want to retch. He covered his mouth and nose with his hand and pressed the button, but nothing happened. He pushed it several more times and then banged it out of frustration. He was forced to accept the fact that he was going to have to climb up six flights of steps. By the time he got to the top he was exhausted. Yvonne had the front door open and was standing outside, with her arms folded.

"What time do you call this?"

"The traffic was really bad," Den said, attempting to squeeze out a plausible excuse while, at the same time, trying to gulp air into his dying lungs.

"There's always traffic and come to think of it there's always an excuse, isn't there? Have you got the kids their presents?"

"What?"

"I said have you got the kids their Christmas presents?"

At this point of their encounter Yvonne was acting like a pressure cooker which had been left boiling at a high temperature for too long and was ready to spew its contents over anyone brave or stupid enough to want to attempt to open the lid. At the same time Den was doing a good impression of an inexperienced cook, unable to get the lid off in time to save its contents.

"Yeah, yeah, of course I have. They're in the errh van," Den said rubbing his nose and looking away.

"You're lying."

"Course I'm not lying," Den said dismissively.

"Well why don't you go downstairs and pick them up, whatever they may be? Fetch them so Freddie and Kevin can open them in front of me."

"I'm not going all the way back down there again, unless it's to leave."

"There's another set of lifts at this end," she said pointing with her thumb over her left shoulder. "They work fine."

While their parents were arguing, Kevin and Freddie sat crouched behind the slightly ajar front door. They had their heads locked together, with one eye each peering through the letterbox. They heard everything that was being said.

"I'm late, you're late, why don't we just do this another time?" Den was trying to keep a lid on the tension that he could feel welling up inside his body.

"I can wait. Seeing my children's faces light up when they have presents from their father is more important than being on time for my friends."

"Well I'm not doing what you tell me to do," replied Den, taking two steps forward and squaring up to Yvonne. They stood still for a moment, glaring at each other. There was little height difference between them.

"You don't frighten me Dennis Malcolm Leslie Johnston," Yvonne said venomously, taking two steps towards her ex-husband. "You've had all week; all month for that matter to go out and find them something. Have you any idea what it means to them? I could buy them a hundred presents…" she said angrily pointing her finger at him "…but the most important one is the one they get from you."

"Don't you point your finger at me or I'll…."

"Or you'll what. Knock the living daylights out of me? Is that what you'll do? You lazy good-for-nothing."

"Don't call me a lazy good-for-nothing."

By this stage the argument had deteriorated into a shouting match where neither of them were listening.

"Do you ever consider your boys' feelings? Well do you?"

"God, I'm here aren't I."

"Yeah very nice of you to turn up, when you feel like it, when it suits you. You swan in and out of their lives…"

"Stop," was the only word that came from in front of them. Den and Yvonne looked down to see Freddie, who'd run out from behind the door and was now standing in between them with his hands outstretched, like a traffic policeman.

"Will you both just stop." There was a momentary pause as both ceased arguing and switched their attention to their nine-year-old son.

"I don't care that much about my present to be honest. I just wanted to spend some time with my dad. That's all I want to do."

*

"Right, where do you two stop-outs want to go shopping then?" Den asked his children, who were squeezed tightly into the front passenger seat of his van.

"Bluewater," they shouted out in unison.

"Ok, well, in recognition of the excellent work you did helping me out of a tricky spot with your mum, you can both spend £20 on your Christmas presents instead of £15, alright."

"Yeah," they shouted out excitedly.

They drove down the A2 and arrived at the Bluewater shopping centre in next to no time. The only slight problem was getting a parking space and when they eventually found one they pulled up, got out and made their way into the shopping centre, via one of the department stores. Den almost bumped into a couple as they struggled through the electric doors, laden with dozens of shopping bags. His mind was elsewhere, on the football match. The commentator on the radio had reported that Arsenal were one nil up at half time. Den had already counted out his winnings.

When he eventually turned round to check on Freddie and Kevin, he realised they were gone. They'd disappeared without a trace and for a split second Den doubted whether he'd turned up with them at all.

"Freddie, Kevin, you little rascals, this isn't the time for playing games," he said, looking behind a display of T-shirts. Perspiration was starting to form on his forehead. He was in enough trouble with

Yvonne as it was. Den had an image flash into his mind of turning up at Yvonne's the next day and her standing in the doorway with her rolling pin, saying 'forgotten something have we?'

"This isn't funny. If you don't come out here right now you're not getting any Christmas presents." As soon as he said this two heads appeared from behind a checkout counter.

"Ok, very good, you thought you had dad tricked there didn't you?"

"Dad can we have some chocolate? Please."

"Yeah, you can have some as long as you don't do that again."

So the first stop was the newsagents, and after two chocolate bars each, Freddie and Kevin were running around the shopping centre like mini-madmen, pumped up to the eyeballs with sugar. Den still only had one thing on his mind.

"I thought we might look in the electrical shop first kids, you know, for your presents, what do you say?" Both Freddie and Kevin weren't listening to their dad. Instead they were watching a young shop assistant demonstrating a toy helicopter. They looked on, transfixed, as it hovered in the air above their heads.

"I want one of those," said Kevin.

"I tell you what, let's pop over to the shop across the way and see if they've got anything in there that you might want to buy. If not we can always come back."

"Ok," they said begrudgingly. Den placed a hand on each of their backs and gently ushered them away. As soon as they got to the shop Den made a beeline for the TV section at the back, but was held up by his kids' reluctance to want to follow him.

"I don't want a telly," complained Freddie eventually, after waiting patiently beside his dad.

"That's good because you don't get much for twenty quid. Hold on for a minute, dad's just waiting for the football scores to come up. Still one nil, get in," said Den. "Right where do you two want to go?"

"Games shop," said Kevin.

"Ok, come on, what are we waiting for?" They made their way

outside the store and then jumped onto the escalator to the upper level. As they approached the computer games shop, Den glanced at the TV screens in the entrance showing the latest war game.

"What about that Kevin? Looks good," asked Den.

"Yeah but that's too expensive dad, you only gave us twenty. That's thirty-five."

"Thirty-five quid for that, blimey things have changed since I was a kid. My whole Atari console didn't cost me that much." Den considered it for a while and to be honest he fancied a go of it himself. He was bored of all the younger kids games the boys had and with the football result going his way, he was feeling generous.

"Do you really want it?"

"Yeah, course I do," replied Kevin. "Bang, bang, bang," he shouted, mimicking the soldiers in the game. He then pretended to shoot Freddie, who obliged by acting like he'd been hit in the chest with a series of bullets. He shook his body before he wobbled around and then collapsed in a heap on the shop floor.

"You do know that mum says I'm not supposed to have things like that at my age."

"Mum says, mum says. Let me tell you son, when I was your age I did a lot of things I wasn't supposed to," explained Den.

"Really, like what?"

"I don't know. Stuff. Like once I remember letting the tyres down on my teacher's bicycle. He ended up having to push it all the way home."

"A kid in my school stabbed one of the teachers."

"Did he? That's not very nice."

"No, it was a girl."

"What, a woman teacher?"

"No dad, a girl who did the stabbing." Den was lost for words. Kevin then asked with his eyes wide open and a frown on his face. "Did you ever steal anything?"

"Me and my gang had been known to do the odd job now and again," Den said boasting.

"It's just that mum says stealing is for losers."

"Does she, well, so do you want this or not?" asked Den changing the subject.

"If you don't mind dad, that'll be wicked."

"Ok," Den said as he strolled up to the counter, reached into his back pocket and handed over forty pounds to the spotty teenager standing at the till.

"This has got some great effects. You made a good choice there," said the boy.

"Oh it's not for me, it's for my son," Den said pointing in the general direction of Kevin. "He loves all that blood and guts stuff."

"What the little kid over there? Yeah, right, mister," said the assistant. Den gave him a disapproving look before he grabbed his change and the bag with the computer game inside.

"Ok lads one down and one to go," said Den as he walked back to his hyperactive children. "Where to Freddie? You lead the way."

"I want to go over there," replied Den's younger son, scanning the general area and pointing to the music shop across the other side of the mall.

"Off we go then," instructed Den. Freddie did as he was told but at breakneck speed, leaving Den and his brother struggling to keep up. Den watched Freddie disappear into the store but eventually found him a few minutes later in the Urban Music section. He was standing in the middle of an aisle holding a CD by an American rapper.

"Can I have this one, please?"

"Let me have a look," said Den. Parental guidance is advised, read the sticker on the front in bold black ink.

"Why not, after all you'll be ten next year, nearly a man."

"What else? You've still got over twenty quid left?" So Freddie led them back upstairs to the DVD's and straight to the horror section. Den had a look through them all with his sons, until Freddie settled on two: Zombies Dawn of the Dead and The Night of The Flesh Eating Monsters.

"Are you sure you want these?"

"If I get two it says they're on special offer."

"Well spotted Freddie," Den said rubbing his shaved head. Look lads, best not tell mum about these, alright. Are we agreed on that?" Freddie and Kevin nodded compliantly.

"Right that's all the presents done. Ok we're just going to go back to the TV shop and check out the final scores."

"Dad," protested Freddie.

"Come on it'll only take five minutes and then we can get something to eat."

"What, burgers and milkshakes?"

"If you want," replied Den, grabbing hold of an arm in each hand and gently dragging his sons out of the record shop. Den waited patiently for the last five minutes of the day's games to be played out. The commentators soon got onto the Arsenal vs Tottenham game.

"We're in for a nail biting finish here at White Hart Lane. Tottenham have equalised and, hold on, the Arsenal striker is clear through on goal. He's just got the keeper to beat. He's chipped him, and no, he's hit the crossbar and it's gone over for a goal kick. That was a real let off for Tottenham who have, with a lot of perspiration and a fair amount of inspiration as well, managed to claw their way back into this game."

Den was about to shout a whole string of expletives when he looked down to his left and saw Freddie staring back up at him, with an angelic expression on his face.

"Damn what bad luck," said Den, putting his clenched fist into his open mouth.

"...and now it's Tottenham's turn to attack. A long ball from the keeper has found the youngster on the wing, he passes it to the Spurs striker, who shoots and scores. The crowd have gone absolutely ballistic. There are scenes of jubilation here at White Hart Lane as Tottenham edge ahead of their arch rivals. The Arsenal players have quickly gathered the ball to restart the game, but there's very little time in fact, yes, there's the final whistle. It appears that in a dramatic local derby, with the last kick of the game, Tottenham have beaten

Arsenal by two goals to one."

"I'm hungry, can we go and eat now?" asked Freddie pulling on the sleeve of Den's leather jacket.

"No son we're going home. I've got a tin of beans in the cupboard."

"But dad you said…"

"Don't argue with me son, just do as you're told."

*

"Here we go, much better than burgers and fries. Good bit of fibre in them beans you know." Freddie and Kevin didn't say a word. They were so hungry by this stage they would have eaten anything, even their dad's burnt beans on toast. There was a moment when all that could be heard was the sound of knives and forks on plates and mouths chomping their way through dinner. Then, out of the blue, in between chews, Kevin asked an unexpected question.

"Do you think you and mum will ever get back together?"

"I'm not sure she'll have me back," Den replied honestly, without giving it too much thought.

"I knew it," said Kevin, in vitriolic fashion to Freddie. "You still like mum, don't you?"

"What's your name? Inspector Morse?" replied Den, looking flustered.

"Who's that?" asked Kevin.

"Never mind." There was a pause as they all carried on eating their food.

"She still likes you," said Freddie, who was precariously balanced on two cushions; it was a makeshift solution to allow him to reach the kitchen table.

"What've I told you about making stuff up Freddie?" said Den.

"She does, honest, I'm not lying," protested Freddie.

"How do you know then?" said Den, smiling at his son to help lighten the mood.

"I caught her looking at a photo, the one of you together on Brighton beach. She keeps it in the bottom drawer of her bedside table." Den didn't know what to say. A lump came to his throat and he felt uncomfortable.

"You shouldn't get your hopes up, I'm not sure if me and your mum could ever work things out."

"You're not drinking anymore, though, are you dad?"

"No, no I'm not."

"Well I reckon if you told her that you still liked her and that things would be different…"

"She'd never believe me," Den said sharply without meaning to. He checked himself and softened his voice.

"I've promised her loads of things in the past and never kept my word. She's got every right not to believe that it would be different this time."

"You've always come and seen us though, that's got to mean something."

"I wasn't always the most responsible dad in the world though, was I? Do you remember the time I left you behind when we got the tube once? Scared the living daylights out of you."

"Yeah, yeah I remember," confirmed Freddie, hanging his head in disappointment.

"Well I've done loads of things like that to your mum. I think that's why she's so angry at me."

"That's alright dad. I just think that mum still likes you, that's all."

"Look, how about watching one of your new DVD's Freddie," Den said, changing the subject.

"Ice cream first," replied Freddie.

"That's right, how could I forget." Den got up from the small kitchen table, went over to the tiny freezer section of his mini-fridge and carefully pulled out the tub of raspberry ripple ice cream.

"Whose are those over there dad?" Kevin asked pointing at the half finished paintings, stacked in a pile, leaning against the wall at the other end of the room.

DENNIS MALCOLM LESLIE JOHNSTON

"They're mine."

"I didn't know you could paint?"

"I can't really, it's, well, it's something I enjoy doing."

"Can I have a go?" asked Kevin.

"Me too," shouted Freddie, not wanting to be left out.

"Finish your ice cream first," Den said as he placed the two bowls in front of them. Within a matter of seconds they'd both scoffed the lot and were struggling to get down from their chairs.

Den obligingly cleared a small area in the corner of his bedsit by the window and set up two easels. He got a mixing palette for them to share and showed them how to blend the colours. Freddie and Kevin watched intently as their dad carefully squeezed the precious oil out of a couple of the tubes and mixed them together to make various shades of greens and blues.

"What should we paint?" asked Freddie eagerly.

"Well either you could, I don't know, look out the window and paint what you see, although perhaps it's a bit too dark. What about something in the flat? Or, you could use your imagination."

"How do we do that?"

"Well what I do is, I close my eyes, take a few deep breaths, imagine I'm looking at a blank screen and then see what comes up." Both his children closed their eyes while Den watched on.

"I don't see anything," said Freddie soon getting frustrated.

"Give it a bit longer."

"Oh I see Santa, on a sleigh being pulled by his reindeer."

"Good. Try to remember what you see and then you can paint it." Den looked through his old cardboard box of paints and pulled out a bright red tube for Santa's coat.

"Wait, I see, I see a dolphin," said Freddie jumping up and down on the spot with his eyes still closed, almost knocking over the lamp on the table next to him.

"Good lad, remember it and then open your eyes," Den said as he caught hold of Freddie, purposely locking his arms by the side of his body, to stop him from doing any damage.

Den then helped them mix the right colours. As they began to paint, Den sat himself down on the floor, between the two easels. He started giving them advice and helping Freddie with the difficult bits.

Without him realising it, the experience became something special, a moment that was timeless, where Den became totally absorbed in his children's enthusiasm and energy. Not once did he think about himself. Not once did he want a drink. Not once did he think about making a bet or about what a terrible father he'd been. Not once.

Chapter 3
The day after Boxing Day – three tears of sadness

"So how was your week, Den?"

"It was sweet, as good as any week can be, really. Well it was alright I suppose, but then, well thinking about it, it didn't really go to plan, no it was pretty bad. Yeah it was bad," Den said, eventually talking himself round to the truth, a place he'd often struggle to be in his life.

"Why, what happened?" The person asking the questions was called Tanya, a gentle, soft spoken woman, in her late forties with long, straight, jet black hair. She had an angular face and was thin; a bit too thin for Den's liking. When she smiled you could see the crow's feet around her eyes which were bright blue, and when she stared at Den he felt like they looked right into his soul.

"Well," Den paused for a bit; he felt uncomfortable telling a group of strangers exactly what happened, "I had an argument with my ex-wife."

"What about?"

"What do you mean?"

"What was your argument about?"

"God, when we argue it doesn't have to be about anything but this time it was because I was late to pick up the kids." Den was slouched down in the chair, with his legs stretched out and crossed at his ankles, staring down at his trainers.

"Did you say you were sorry?"

"Well of course I did," Den lied. Tanya nodded but didn't feel the need to reply.

"She made me lose my temper."

"How did she do that?"

"She does this thing where she calls me by my middle names."

"Go on."

"She called me Dennis Malcolm Leslie Johnston." At that point Den felt like the dozen or so people in the room with him, who were sitting on old school chairs, arranged in a circle, were sniggering at him.

"How did that make you feel?" asked Britney, who was sitting to Den's left. You wouldn't believe it to look at her but she was young, only twenty-one or twenty-two. Her hair was bleached, an unnatural yellowy blond, and it was messy. Her eyes had thick black lines under them, like she'd smoked fifty cigarettes a day for the last ten years and hadn't slept properly for months. Her face was drawn out and her skin a light grey colour. She sat with her legs crossed and her hands wedged between them because sometimes they shook so much she couldn't control them. It was like they vibrated; in tune with the chords of her discomfort.

"I felt like punching her lights out, didn't I."

"And after that?" asked Tony. He was a middle-aged man, sitting across the circle from Den. He had an enormous round belly, which was so big that if he balanced a cup of coffee on it, he wouldn't have to bend his head more than a few inches to take a sip.

"Like I needed a drink". This brought a wry smile to Tanya's face and a ripple of agreement from the others. Den looked like he was going to say something else but hesitated. He was finding it difficult to take the next step. No one else spoke. It was as if they were observing the class etiquette, with everyone in the room realising that these few minutes were about Den and that it would be their turn soon.

"And then I felt, bad, sort of guilty". He looked up from his feet and stared into Tanya's eyes.

"Guilty?" asked Tanya in a soothing, almost hypnotic voice. But the inclination in her tone hid the probing pressure that was behind her question.

"Since I've been sober, well, I've had time to think about things. How I treated my wife. The times I lost my temper, the times I lost my temper at her. The times I shouted at my, at my..." and for the first time since he could remember, Den lost control of his emotions. He put his hand up to his face in an attempt to shield his tears from the other members of the group. There was a long silence before Britney finally stretched over and gently began rubbing his left shoulder. He took a deep breath.

"I just don't think I've been a very good dad," Den said choking on the words a little, while he was still rubbing his eyes.

"It's alright Dennis," said Tanya, "this is an important breakthrough. Not much good usually comes of getting angry at people. Either they mirror us and are angry back, or they take that anger inwards and get upset by it. Acknowledging how you've made other people feel and learning to respect their emotions are key steps in your path to life without alcohol." She paused as if waiting for her words to sink in.

"The next stage, Dennis, is to say you're sorry, to those people that you've hurt the most during the time you spent being the old you. Then you must learn to forgive yourself." Her words seemed to help stem Den's tears. It was as if he could see a light, a glimmer of hope at the end of the tunnel of despair. Britney handed him a small crumpled piece of tissue, which he used to wipe his eyes. They gave him a few minutes to compose himself.

"I'm alright now, thanks."

"We're all very proud of you for sharing that with us Dennis." The group broke into a disjointed and short-lived round of applause with a few people saying the odd 'well done' and 'nice one'. Tanya then turned to Britney.

"Now Britney, how has your week been?"

*

Despite dozens of meetings it was the first time Den had ever cried. Now he was having trouble snapping out of the glum mood he was in, the one that he'd opened himself up to. On top of that he felt paranoid; like he must have looked stupid in front of everyone.

The AA meeting finished at eight o'clock. Den's van was in the garage, something to do with the alternator, and he didn't have much time to get from Greenwich to the other side of Lewisham. Luckily Britney offered to give him a lift. Den was grateful: it would have been cold outside waiting for a bus.

"You did really well today," she said, glancing at him.

"Thanks," he replied while staring out of the car window, watching the shops go by.

"It can't be easy for a strong, silent type like you, to open up like that." While she was driving, she was also struggling with a packet of cigarettes that were in the side door of her car. She finally pulled a Benson from the gold packet. Den offered her a light.

"Oh you're a real gentlemen, thank you." They'd stopped at a set of traffic lights. She took her right hand off the wheel and held his wrist to steady the flame, glancing up several times to check if the lights had changed. Den knew she was flirting with him. In the past he might have been tempted to take this relationship further, but something had changed. It wasn't because she was a real mess: serious issues with her father, as well as being an alcoholic and a drug addict. The truth was he wanted to get back with his ex-wife. That was one of the reasons for going to these meetings. The other one was for his boys.

"I was wondering. No, you probably wouldn't want to. Don't worry." Den kept quiet, hoping that she would leave it there. Unfortunately his silence seemed to encourage her.

"It's just that, ok, look, I'm going to come right out with it. Would you like to go out with me one night?"

"What, for a drink?"

"No silly". She suddenly went all girlie and wobbly. She started revealing her age, and more to the point, how needy she was. Then she laughed and it sounded like someone had let off a machine gun.

"What then?"

"I don't know, just a night out to the cinema or something."

"I don't really like movies and anyway you're not my type."

"What do you mean I'm not your type? So what is your type?" He was playing with her. He didn't have much respect for women, especially when they were so needy.

"You're not hairy enough for me."

"You're winding me up, right?"

"No seriously, I like my women hairy. Hairy armpits, hairy legs, hairy chest, the hairier the better."

"Ugghh, she said, that's completely weird." It had the required impact. Den was hoping Britney would back off if she heard this. It would have been a bit of a nightmare for Den if she hadn't, because he hated hairy women as much as the next guy. But at least this way he would be letting her down gently, and hopefully, that meant he could still get a lift off her again, if he was ever in trouble. There was a short pause in the conversation. Den began listening to the radio.

"I noticed that you never talk about your parents much at the meetings."

"Yeah, well, there's nothing much to say." Den was abrupt, so as to give her a clear message.

"Don't you have much to do with them anymore?" She said this and then took a long drag on her cigarette, breathing the smoke back out through her nose.

"No, no I don't," he said getting annoyed.

"Sorry, just asking."

"Thanks for the interest. I'm just over here by the way, next left. You can drop us at the top of this road if you want."

*

"Den, that is really good."

"Don't talk rubbish," Den replied. His response gave away the fact that he wasn't used to receiving compliments.

"No honestly dear, I've been coming to painting classes for years and I've never seen anything as distinctive and well, as pleasing on the eye as that." The little grey haired old lady, who was one of the nicest people Den had met, was standing to the right of his easel studying his painting. He could feel himself getting embarrassed, the heat rising in his cheeks as more of the class took notice of what Dorothy was saying.

"Let's have a butcher's" said Charlie, who was sitting at an easel to the left of Den. He got up and shuffled round to look from the other side to where Dorothy was standing. A slim, middle-aged woman had come in to model for them. She was partially naked, sitting with her feet crossed and her knees tucked up to her chest. Draped round her shoulders was a beige shawl.

Den had quite an individual painting style when it came to still life. He would make an outline of the person or object using charcoal or a dark pencil and would then start to fill it in with oil paint, but would only complete perhaps one half or two thirds.

"Have you ever thought of selling your work?" asked Charlie.

"No of course not, it's just a bit of therapy really."

"I'm serious, I reckon if you went somewhere posh; up west or even local perhaps around Blackheath or Greenwich, you'd find a buyer for that."

"I think Charlie's got a good point" said Denise the class teacher, who'd quietly walked behind Den without him noticing.

Their compliments gave Den a strange, unfamiliar feeling. It wasn't the kind of false sense of security that he got from getting drunk. This was different. After so many years of being told he wouldn't amount to anything, this was a defining moment, where he felt like he'd done something right for once; something that wasn't at anyone else's expense. He looked round, at the faces of the three people gazing at his painting and he felt a sense of admiration. Like he was, in some small way, responsible for making them feel happy. For once it wasn't so much about him, how he felt or what he wanted. Instead it was about him giving something to other people.

"Right, that's all we have time for today," announced Denise. On hearing her words the small crowd that had gathered around Den's painting, quickly dispersed. "I'd like you all to thank Erica for modelling for us tonight." There was a gentle round of applause from the class in acknowledgement.

"That's it for this term. For those of you interested in coming next year, we will be starting off by looking at some of the great modernist painters. I want you to think about what kind of style you might want to adopt and I'm going to get those of you who are interested to try out quite a few different techniques that will be new to most of you. Ok, thank you all very much, you've all done really well. Have a happy New Year."

Den was so proud of his painting that rather than storing it with the rest of the class's stuff in the back room of the community centre, he decided to take it home with him. His small bedsit in Lewisham was only ten minutes' walk away. He tipped the painting on its side, as some of the oil paint hadn't dried properly and was careful to hold it away from his body.

"I meant what I said Dennis, that's good work you've done there."

"Thanks. Don't worry, I'll remember you when I'm rich and famous."

"Have a happy New Year," said Denise smiling.

"You too," he replied as he walked out of the community centre with a spring in his step. It was a cold evening and he'd wished he'd remembered his scarf. The weather forecasters had promised snow but it hadn't arrived yet. He wanted to grab the sides of his brown leather jacket and pulled them in tight at the top but was having to hold his painting with both hands. As he walked down Lewisham High Street he became distracted by some of the Christmas displays in the shop windows.

"Watch it," said Den. It was a reflex reaction to the person who'd just bumped into him and almost knocked the painting out of his hand.

"Who are you telling to watch it?" The reply came from a young kid wearing a thick, black sweatshirt with the hood up, underneath a waist high, black leather jacket. Den quickly noticed that the youth wasn't alone. Standing on the pavement next to him were three other boys. None of them could have been more than sixteen years old.

"Who do you think?" But Den certainly didn't think; instead the red mist, that had been such a problem for most of his life, descended in an instant. "Donald Duck?"

What Den hoped to achieve by this comment was hard to say. We all want a bit of respect but this probably wasn't the time, or the place, or the best way for Den to try and get some. The teenager didn't bother to come up with a clever reply; he just pulled out a flick knife, pressed the button and in one motion went to stab Den in the chest.

Luckily Den saw it coming but only had a fraction of a second to react. He pushed the painting out in front of him, using it as a shield to protect himself. The youth was coming at him with such energy that the knife ripped straight through the canvas like it wasn't there. Den stepped back, holding the painting out with his left hand, forcing it down towards the pavement to catch the teenager off balance. He then let go of the painting, turned and punched the youth in the face with his clenched right fist. He didn't make a full contact, his blow glancing off the side of his cheek. It was enough to make the boy drop his knife as he fell backwards onto the pavement. Unfortunately he took the painting with him. In a frantic attempt to get his hand free, the youth smashed the painting on the ground. In the meantime Den quickly picked up the knife before any of the youth's friends had a chance to intervene.

There was a brief stand off. One of them spat at him. The boy who'd tried to stab Den kicked the broken painting in his direction. They then slowly backed off and started to walk away.

"Be seeing you Mr Duck. Quack, quack, quack." All four of them made quacking noises and started to laugh. Den could feel his heart pounding in his chest. The vapours pouring out of his mouth were so thick it looked like he was smoking. He bent down and picked up the broken remains of the painting, which he'd so lovingly created but which had so easily been destroyed. His head dropped in despair and he slowly made his way back to his bedsit, clutching the pieces of wood and torn canvas in his hands.

Chapter 4
28th December – four American tourists

"I have a question."

"Yes, sonny?" Den put on his best fake smile. This kid was really trying his patience. He was almost into double figures. What little Brady should have said was, I have a list of questions as long as my arm and I'm never going to stop until you've answered every one in the most ridiculous amount of detail possible.

"My names not 'sonny', it's Brad," Brad said in the most polite way he could, which meant he still came across as a 'know-it-all'. Den was quickly growing to dislike this son of Satan, who looked like the winner of the American National Spelling competition. His glasses were so thick that when he looked up his eyes appeared to be the size of golf balls. He wore geeky looking clothes, with the matching rucksack and baseball cap finishing the look off nicely. His sister wasn't much better.

"Ok, what do you want to know?"

"How did Green-witch get its name?"

"Well, Brad, that's a good question. But, for starters, in England we say 'Gren-itch', not 'Green-witch'. 'Gren' as in rhymes with Sir Christopher Wren rather than the colour 'green'. " Den said this in the most condescending way he knew how." You know, the man who designed the Houses of Parliament."

"Don't you mean St. Pauls Cathedral?" replied Brad

"That's right little Brady, no flies on you today. Mr Wren designed that as well."

"We have a Greenwich in America" said Brad's mother.

"Really," replied Den, in a disbelieving way.

"Well two actually, Greenwich Village in New York and Greenwich in Connecticut."

"So you must be familiar with how it originally got its name."

"No, no I'm not," she said looking a bit upset.

"Anyway where was I? Yes and we say 'itch' like an itch that you want to scratch. Having said that, Greenwich originally got its name from witches in the 14th century, so your mistake is, well, understandable." Den laughed an awkward, tense laugh but soon stopped when he realised Brad's parents weren't joining in. "Well these witches were brought over from Ireland during the, erm, great potato famines and were burnt at the stake at the top of the park. They were often dressed in green robes, hence Green Witches, Greenwich."

"But I thought that the name originated from Saxon times when it was a village market surrounded by green fertile farming land. 'Wic' back then meant village market. So it was the 'village market on the green' or green wic."

"No, I think you must have got your facts muddled up there," Den said, while patting him on the head. He then gave him a clip round the ear when the other family members weren't looking.

"Hey," complained Brad. Luckily his voice was drowned out by a passing bus.

"What about Blackheath?" Brad said, clearly wanting to exact his revenge verbally; making Den fumble for an explanation.

"Everybody knows that it got its name from the black death..."

"Wrong." Brad then made the noise of a buzzer in a TV quiz show when the contestant gets the answer incorrect.

"It's because..." Brad said, once again trying to steal Den's thunder.

"Now, on your left we have the main building of what was originally Greenwich Hospital. It was taken over in 1873 to be a Royal Naval College. Now, of course, it is occupied by Greenwich University," Den said speaking very quickly, in an attempt to freeze out his annoying co-host.

"Let the boy speak," interrupted Brad's father who, up until this point, had been fairly passive. Den kept quiet.

"Good, go on Brad," his father prompted.

"...back in olden times it was called Blackheath because it was a bleak and inhospitable place, hence the name 'bleak heath'."

"What about the Cutty Sark?" Asked Brad's father.

"What about it?" replied Den, defensively.

"Where did it get its name from?"

Den knew this one but he just couldn't remember, so once again he made something up.

"Well as I told you the, errh, Cutty Sark was originally used to transport tea from China. Now, back then in the 1870's a slang name for tea was 'sark', and 'cutty' well, that was a word used to describe the way the tea was prepared when it got to England. They would put it in this tall…"

"I thought it originated from a poem by Robbie Burns in which he describes a cutty sark as a short nightdress and this is shown on the figurehead of the ship which is wearing a cutty sark."

"Well that's a good point Brat, I mean Brad," knowing his slip wasn't too far wide of the mark. He had to think quickly. "It's true there are some people who believe that this is the case." He looked up and noticed that a group of teenagers were walking towards them. They all moved into single file to make room. Den held back. Brad walked on ahead slightly. His parents and Brad's sister were in front of him. When they weren't looking, Den did what he thought was best given the circumstances, and tripped Brad up. He used to do it when he was at school; clip other kids back feet when they were walking in front of him. They would normally stumble and look a bit silly. Only on rare occasions would they fall over. How was he to know it would work so well on little Brady? The boy went flying, front first onto the pavement.

Den had never heard such a little cry baby in his life. As far as he was concerned it was only a few scratches. Well, the one on his knee did bleed for a bit, but it was nothing a couple of stitches wouldn't sort out. Then Brad started accusing Den of doing it on purpose, which he denied, of course. Luckily, he was almost at the end of his tour. He waited for a bit but when he realised they weren't going to give him a tip, he moved back to his pitching point. This was outside the ice rink that had temporarily been put up over Christmas time, in the grounds of the University, in between the two chapels.

*

"Tours of Greenwich, tours of Green-witch, anyone. Can I interest you lovely ladies in a tour of this magnificent and historic part of London?"

"No thanks, we only live round the corner," replied the girl closest to Den, out of the group of three.

"I bet you didn't know how Greenwich got its name?"

"No we don't, we're not bovvered either," the three girls said the last few words in unison.

Den had only been doing it a few weeks. It was hard going but he was trying to stay positive. He reckoned that, come the summer, he could get as many as thirty people at a time to go on a tour. At £5 each plus tips, he was onto a winner. Then he wouldn't have to do any more jobs with Jack. No more selling stolen electrical gear. No more scrimping and scraping to make ends meet.

"Is that you Den?"

"Who wants to know?" Den replied to the short, balding man who was standing in front of him. He looked a bit like an East End gangster who'd fallen on hard times.

"It's me, Jimmy from school. I haven't seen you for what, nearly twenty years."

"Yes it's got to be something like that," Den replied, struggling to recall the face.

"We had a laugh back in them days, didn't we?"

"Yes," replied Den but if enthusiasm was energy, he barely had enough to punch his way out of a paper bag.

"Do you remember old Duffer Robertson, our Maths teacher? When you let the tyres down on his bicycle and he had to push it all the way home. What did we used to call him?"

"Rocket Robbo," said Den breaking into a smile.

"That's it, The Rocket, 'cos you managed to put that Bunsen burner under his metal chair once. I remember it as if it was yesterday. When he sat down on it he must have jumped ten foot in the air."

"So did you ever get hitched?"

"Yeah, I married Yvonne, Yvonne Wainwright."

"Not Yvonne, from Trafalgar Road."

"That's the one."

"You old dog, she was lovely, legs up to her arm pits. I used to like her."

"What about you?" Den had already forgotten the man's name and wouldn't be able to remember it if his life depended on it.

"Divorced."

"Bad luck."

"You win some, you lose some. Bit of a nasty separation to be honest but I don't want to bore you with the gory details." Den gave him a 'you're probably right not to bore me' expression.

"She ran off with an Italian waiter that worked in the restaurant in Deptford High Street. Fleeced me for every penny I had. Got the house, the car, everything."

"How did she get all the money, if she left you?"

"Well, she tricked me didn't she. Been planning the whole thing for years. Stashing money away. Then I lost my temper one night, held her at knife point; police got involved an' all that. I ended up in prison for six months. She said I never paid her any attention. Said I thought more about my dog Bruno than I did her."

"Prison?" Den said, almost breaking into a smile at the thought of finally meeting someone who'd made a worse mess of their own life than he had. He'd had a few brushes with the law, more than he'd care to mention, but like a cat with nine lives he'd always managed to get away without a conviction. Den's unplanned school reunion then became a bit difficult when its main attendant broke down and began to sob.

"Life goes on though eh," Den said, thinking twice about patting him on the back.

"Not really, I haven't got a penny to my name now."

"What about a job?"

"I used to be a car mechanic, garage in Deptford, but they sacked me when I was put inside. That's when they moved into the house. Our house. I guess I never appreciated what I had, you know? You promise me one thing." As he said this Jimmy put his hand on Den's shoulder and lent into him. Den couldn't avoid being exposed to the overpowering stench of alcohol and stale tobacco mixed together on his breath. "Promise me that you'll cherish your missus." And like the hundreds of drunken conversations which Den had had over the years with strangers in pubs and at bus stops, just like them, he found himself placating this sad alcoholic.

"I promise mate."

"No, you've got to mean it," Jimmy said grabbing Den with both hands and pulling him closer.

"Yes I promise," replied Den. But what Den's old school friend didn't realise was that this time, Den really did mean what he said.

*

Den had pretty much given up with the tours for the day. It was getting cold and the light was fading fast. He watched from a distance as a man, who was clearly going too fast and trying to be flash, crashed into a girl and they ended up in a heap on the ice together.

It probably looked worse than it was, he thought. He couldn't see them clearly but from what he could make out, they looked like they were getting on well together. Not that he had any sudden urge to get knocked over on an ice rink. But it made him get in touch with a feeling, like there was something missing in his life. He'd often thought it was his dad, but he wasn't sure. He'd taken Den ice skating a couple of times when he was young. Perhaps that was it.

Then he had a realisation as he looked on—at all the people with their friends and family circling round and round on the ice rink— with smiles on their faces or expressions of surprise or anxiety at near misses or wobbles. They looked like people who loved Christmas and Den wished that he could be one of them.

"Dad, dad."

Den turned round to see his younger son, Freddie, running towards him. He knelt down and Freddie jumped straight into Den's arms. Den gave him a hug and held on, like he never wanted to let go. He was warm, as if he'd just come out of the bath. Close behind was Kevin and when he joined the two of them, he almost knocked them all over.

"What are you up to?"

"Mum promised that she'd take us ice skating," said Kevin who looked more like Den everyday. He had clear blue eyes, a square looking jaw and a button nose. His hair was mousy brown and short. Freddie was definitely more like Yvonne, with his green eyes, pale complexion and high cheek bones.

Den glanced up and saw Yvonne coming up behind them. There was an anxious moment, a standoff between them, as Den's ex-wife sized him up. Her expression was stern and cold.

"What are you doing here?" Yvonne said, folding her arms in front of her.

"I've started giving guided tours".

"Do me a favour," Yvonne said almost breaking into a smile. "What do you know about Greenwich?"

"I know that it got its name from Saxon times when it was called the Green Port and that this place here...," he said pointing to the grand white washed Georgian buildings with large sash windows either side of him, "...used to be part of Greenwich hospital."

"The next minute you'll be telling me that you're completely off the booze and you want to spend more time with your kids".

That was Yvonne for you, no messing around. There was no point in Den trying to explain to her that he was. She wouldn't believe him. He couldn't blame her, it wasn't the first time he'd tried to pack it in. Den looked at her and hoped that she wasn't going to be tough on him. He deserved all he got, the way he'd treated her but he really wanted to go ice skating with his kids.

"Can dad come?" asked Freddie. He'd loosened his grip and twisted round to face his mum.

"Well that depends, does dad want to come?" Freddie then turned to Den, as if watching a game of tennis from an awkward position.

"Yes, I really do as it happens."

"Well, in that case, I'm sure you won't mind treating your family, will you?"

"I guess not" Den said quickly fumbling in his back pocket to make sure he still had the £20 note he'd got from the American family.

"Thanks mum," shouted Freddie.

Yvonne was a changed woman from the quiet timid mouse that he'd married twelve years ago. Now she wouldn't let anyone mess her around. Nothing got past her, unless she wanted it to, and she was as tough as they came. One thing's for sure though, she loved her boys and he could never fault her for that. He had a lot of respect for her, for what she did for them. He just wished she'd give him some back for what he was trying to do now. Freddie grabbed hold of his dad's hand and started leading Den off to the pay booth, while Kevin and Yvonne stopped to have a quick look at the skaters.

"I wished we might meet you dad," said Freddie.

"That's funny, because I wished for it too," Den replied, with a broad grin on his face. "So do you think you're going to be alright skating?" he said putting his arm round Freddie's shoulders.

"What do you mean? We've been loads of times. It's mum's Christmas treat every year and Uncle Terry, he used to take us all the time."

"Oh right, yes, I forgot about Uncle Terry. Ok, well, go easy on me then."

Uncle Terry was Yvonne's special friend for a while, about two years ago, but it didn't work out. Den never asked why, he was just glad to see the back of him. He always used to say, if you ever want to know what it's like to feel rejected, hurt, angry and frustrated all at once—like you've never felt before—then watch your kids with another man. Watch him as he moves into the life you used to have.

Yvonne and Kevin caught up with them in the queue for the boots. They waited for their turn but the kids were restless. Their excitement had been building up all day and it wasn't released until they got out onto the ice. Den let them go first and then held on tightly to the railing which went round the outside of the rink. As he clung on, he watched them go round and round, laughing and racing each other. Yvonne wasn't bad at all; she had good balance and didn't try and go too fast or be too flashy. After a while Freddie and Kevin skated up to their dad and grabbed hold of his hands, one on either side, and led him out into the middle of the ice rink.

Den thought he must have looked stupid, like a drunk circus clown. He lost his balance more times than he could remember but the boys kept on supporting him and Freddie showed him how it was done, giving Den some good tips. Then, after plenty of warning and words of encouragement they let go, and for a brief moment Den felt like he'd cracked it.

"Watch out Torvill & Dean", he said to the boys as he began to glide on the ice. Unfortunately his moment of glory was brief. He hit a patch of ice that was worn out and his skates got stuck under his feet. He bent forward and then backwards, before he lost his balance and fell heavily on his back. It hurt so much he started to cough but the coughing soon turned to laughter. The thing was, once he'd started, he couldn't stop and neither could Yvonne and the boys. They laughed so much people started staring at them, wondering what the fuss was all about, but they didn't care. It was even funnier when Den got up and did exactly the same thing again, a few seconds later. He hadn't had so much fun in years, probably since the last time he went ice skating, with his dad when he was eight years old.

Chapter 5
29th December – five gold scams

"Money back? What do you mean you want your money back? This ain't Currys, you know. There's always a risk with hooky gear, you know that more than anyone. Call yourself a businessman," said Jack, his arms folded tightly in front of his chest. He was propping himself up against their blue transit van, which had the name of a cable TV company embossed all over it. They were both standing in a lock-up garage. Den was squaring up to his cousin.

"The microwaves you sold me exploded. Do I have to spell it out to you? Kaboom." Den made a motion with both his hands to illustrate the action of a large explosion. "I'm still picking Christmas pud out of my hair." Jack desperately tried not to laugh at the thought of Den covered from head to toe in Christmas pudding. He lowered his head and put his hand over his mouth.

"I suppose you find this funny then do you?" Den said trying not to laugh himself.

"You know the same thing happened to Keith." This was too much for Jack, who couldn't hold it in any longer and started laughing.

"Why what happened to Keith?" he said doubled up.

"Well I phoned up everyone else in time, luckily, but Keith's stupid wife was on the dog and bone. Anyway, I go round there and knock on the door but no one was in, so I thought they must be round someone else's house…"

"Go on," Jack said getting excited.

"Then I clock that the side gate is open and I sneak in and get the whole show, don't I. Keith and Cathy both got splatted at close range. Afterwards they looked like, well, like they'd been dragged out of the sewers or something, like brown snowmen."

"Did he see you?"

"No I don't think so. He'll be after me though at some point. You see this is your short sightedness, cuz. Because of you I've upset another valued customer."

"What do you mean valued? Keith's never paid for anything in his life and what do you mean by another one?"

"Don't you remember the DVD players, those recordable ones you sold me. Top of the line, you said, I do believe they are worth two hundred quid a piece."

"Yeah, what about them?"

"They didn't record anything, you wingnut," Den said flicking Jack's forehead with his finger.

"It's not my fault the gear don't work," Jack said laughing again.

"Well whose fault is it?"

"I've told you before it's them pesky orientals," he explained.

"We are rehsponsbull for all rubbish ehlectronics," Jack said.

"It's not funny."

"Come on Den lighten up you misery."

"I'm just sick of stealing to make ends meet. I don't want to push our luck using this scam either."

"I agree. How many more times do you think we can get away with it? We don't want to be too greedy," said Jack.

"That's rich coming from you," Den said, slapping Jack's big belly.

"Well five is my lucky number."

"Ok, one more then. Which part of London's rich and famous haven't we pillaged from yet?"

"Well we've done Kensington, Chelsea and Hampstead. Let me see…," Jack said picking up a copy of the A to Z which was balanced precariously on the edge of an upturned metal barrel. It was something they'd been using as a makeshift table.

"What about somewhere more central, like Marylebone."

"Ya that's very up-and-coming, full of hurray Henrys," Den said in a posh accent.

"Ya, so I've heard," Jack replied mimicking him.

"Same routine. Is the equipment ready?"

"Yep."

"And this time, I'll do all the talking."

"What have I done wrong this time?"

"Well maestro," teased Den, "you do have a track record of mucking things up. Remember the time you pretended to be David Blaine's brother."

"What was wrong with that?"

"Well he's a Yank for starters."

"Yeah, but…"

"Ahh," Den said holding his hand up, "what about that argument you got into with that kid who'd sussed out what you'd done, which wasn't that hard as you'd hidden that woman's necklace in your overall pocket? Look, my point is, it's all about keeping a low profile. Get in, don't do or say anything memorable, get the job done and get out again. Do you think, 'Jack Blaine', you can manage that this time?"

"Yes alright, no need to go on. Now do you mind if I have something to eat before we go?"

"Ok but get a move on will you."

"I really fancy some dessert. I was going to warm up one of those mini Christmas puds in the microwave. Do you want one?"

*

"So would you describe yourself as a brandy butter man or a double cream sort of person?"

"Shut your Christmas cake hole and scramble that signal for me will you."

"Easy there cuz, you're a bit quick tempered this afternoon." They were sitting on upturned wooden boxes in the back of their blue transit van. Den had parked out of sight of traffic on the main road, positioning the van on a relatively quiet street in front of a row of expensive looking houses near Marylebone High Street. Jack had a laptop computer resting on his knees.

"There we go, nearly done," Jack said furiously pressing the keys. "Give them a few minutes and then we can go in and deliver the normal chat."

"Nice one cuz."

"You up for a beer after," asked Jack without thinking.

"How many times, I'm on the wagon, that's spelt w-a-g-o-n , I don't drink anymore."

"Come on it's me you're talking to, not your wife. One cerveza won't do any harm. That's spelt c-e-r-," Jack paused, unable to spell the rest of the word.

"Just to let you know that the whole spelling out thing loses its impact if you can't actually spell the word you're trying to empahsise. Anyway it's my ex-wife and the answer's the same whoever's asking."

"Talking of ex-wives how is she by the way?" Jack asked.

"Well I…," Den said hesitating. He was unsure whether or not Jack was the right person to talk to, but it didn't take him too much time to realise he had few alternatives. "…was wondering if you could give me a bit of advice on the relationship front."

"I'll have to stop you there cuz. To be honest with you, if it's a matter of physical discomfort then, given that I've suffered from most ailments know to the medical profession, I feel qualified to give out such advice. But if it's a matter of emotional discomfort, affairs of the heart, then you're better off asking someone else. I'd be a hypocrite, given that my own personal life has been a series of shallow, tragic affairs, which undoubtedly would have given Shakespeare a dozen or so more plays to keep us entertained for many centuries to come."

Den initially said nothing, his mouth was left open, a gaping hole in the shape of an almost perfect circle.

"You can be so weird sometimes, do you know that?"

"Some may say weird. Others, the more polite amongst us, might say troubled, like perhaps how a genius might find life a series of abstract illusions, or perhaps a thinker. In fact people would often say to me, Jack you think too much that's your problem."

Den stuck his hand up in the air, partly to stop the relentless noise that was emanating from his relative's mouth and partly to signal that it was time for them to leave the van and get down to business.

"Enough. Come on, let's get this over and done with."

"Ok keep your hair on, what little there is."

"Nice one, thanks for reminding me. You got the wigs?" asked Den.

"Yes they're over here," said Jack, reaching over to pull out a white plastic bag which was stuck behind a pile of old rope. He rummaged around inside and soon pulled out several wigs, one with brown curly hair, one that culminated in a pony-tail at the back, and yet another with straight blond hair. Some had matching moustaches. They both picked the ones they preferred. Once on, they made them look like something out of a 1970s TV drama programme. They climbed out of the back of the van and then pulled out two tool boxes. Den put them on the ground and carefully locked the back door, trying not to draw any attention from the people walking along the pavement.

"Remember I'll do the talking" reiterated Den. As a result Jack held back and waited for Den to be the first to go to the door. Then, when he thought he wasn't looking, he made mouthing movements with his hand in a display of petulance, like he was wearing a glove puppet.

"Oi wingnut, I can see you in the window," Den said as he rang the doorbell, which made a grand chiming sound. The door opened almost straight away and a short middle-aged man answered, wearing a crisp, clean white dressing gown. Initially, he was distracted as he tried to tie the towelling belt around his waist.

"Can I help you?" the man finally said in an extremely posh voice.

"We have been asked," Den said trying to mirror the man's accent "to conduct a free check on your cable equipment to ensure that it is in proper working order. Did you get the letter?"

"Letter? No my wife normally deals…"

"Those people at head office…" said Den, turning towards Jack, "… how many times 'ave we told 'em," he explained, his accent slipping somewhat.

"A million times Leslie, a million times," replied Jack. Den immediately threw Jack a warning glance. As soon as they walked through the front entrance, Den and Jack were on the look out for the most likely hiding place for any valuables.

"The TV's in here," said the owner, leading them down the hallway, through the first door on the right and into the lounge.

Standing to the left of the TV and dominating the already striking room was an eight-foot Christmas tree. Den couldn't help but stare in admiration.

"That's some tree you got there. Scandinavian Blue, if I'm not mistaken."

"I have no idea to be honest. Now you'll have to excuse me: I've just got to sort out a few things, so can I leave you in here for a few minutes?"

"Before you go, I just wanted to know where I can find the toilet?" asked Den.

"Oh the one downstairs is broken at the moment. You'll have to use the one at the top of the stairs, turn right, second door on the left."

"And sorry, one last thing, could you just turn the TV on for us please," Den asked.

"Certainly." The man grabbed hold of the remote control on the

THE TWELVE DAYS OF CHRISTMAS

coffee table and switched it on. When the screen came to life the picture was fuzzy, with zigzag lines shooting across it.

"Look at that, good job we were in the area, isn't it mister errh…"

"Mr Hamilton. I don't understand, it was fine last night."

"We've been having some network problems but they've only been affecting a few small pockets of London," explained Jack.

"I see, well this is a problem. How long will it take you to get it fixed?"

"No time at all sir, you just leave it with us. We'll make sure you're sorted out, good and proper."

*

Den eased the heavy wooden Victorian door open and slowly crept inside the room. Glancing round he saw a large, dark, wooden four-poster bed, which had beige curtain material that draped down from the top, completely concealing the mattress. At the far corner of the room stood a vanity desk with two drawers and a mirror perched on top. Den made his way towards it, while trying to be as quiet as possible.

On arriving at the dresser he glanced at himself in the mirror and felt a tinge of guilt as he carefully pulled open the top drawer. Inside was an inscribed silver box, "To my loving wife: I will treasure you always and forever, stallion."

Not really a modest person by the sounds of it, thought Den, as he grabbed the jewellery box with both hands, flipped the catch and prised it open. His eyes feasted on its contents, which were absolutely jammed inside. Den quickly cupped his right hand, poured roughly half the contents out and then transferred the goods to the left pocket of his overalls. He repeated the motion until the jewellery box was empty, but this time, filling up his other pocket. He carefully placed the box in the drawer and then made his way back across the room. His heart, which was already pounding in his chest, almost missed a beat when a loose floorboard groaned and squealed in

DENNIS MALCOLM LESLIE JOHNSTON

discomfort as he applied pressure.

"Is that you, stallion?" came the muffled voice of a well spoken woman from the bed. Den took a deep breath in. He was rooted to spot, his mind on overdrive. There was silence for what seemed like an eternity before Den finally summoned up the strength to say something.

"Yes dear. I errh need to go to the kitchen," he said trying to impersonate Mr Hamilton.

But before the woman had a chance to answer, Den had sprinted across the space to the door and was out into the hallway. He instinctively looked left and then right before making his way down the stairs. When he reached the bottom, he almost had another heart attack when he inadvertently bumped into Mr Hamilton, who was making his way back towards the lounge.

"Find it alright did you?"

"Find what?"

"The toilet, my dear boy."

"Yes, yes of course, where else would I go?"

"I have no idea." Mr Hamilton said, looking Den up and down suspiciously.

"Anyway best be getting on with things."

"What's that?" Mr Hamilton said pointing at Den's right pocket. Dangling out the side was a gold necklace.

"Oh nothing." Den replied fumbling with the gold chain, quickly pushing it back into his pocket.

"Right I'll, I just need to, to go and sort something out," Mr Hamilton said looking concerned. They both bolted in opposite directions: Mr Hamilton towards the telephone in the kitchen to phone the police and Den to get Jack so they could leave the place as quickly as possible. On entering the lounge he saw Jack talking to a foreign looking middle-age woman who had a feather duster in her hand.

"…and that is the magic of illusion as my brother would always say."

"Jack. Jack."

"What, I wasn't doing anything."

"They're onto us. Grab the bags." For once Jack did as he was told, stooping down to pick up the tool bags and leaving the bemused cleaner to do her feather dusting. In double quick time he followed Den out through the hallway and the front door. Den opened up the back of the van for Jack to throw the tools in. They ran round and jumped in the front seats. Den then had to struggle to pull out some of the jewellery from his pockets, which he threw on Jack's lap, before he could find the keys to the van. At the same time both were glancing around to see if there was anything happening outside.

"I'm getting too old for this," Den said as he finally found the right key and shoved it in the ignition. The engine fired up with a roar, Den slammed his foot on the accelerator and the van sped off, making a loud screeching noise. They weaved their way down a few roads before jumping the lights at the end of James Street and turning left onto Oxford Street.

"Looks like I'll be keeping my lucky number," said Jack.

"Why's that?"

"This stuff has got to be worth a small fortune."

Chapter 6
30th December – six double whiskeys

"The look on your boat race. We've been rumbled, grab your bags," Jack said doing an impression of Den. He then laughed making a strong, loud, hearty chuckling noise, how you might expect Santa Claus to sound if he found something amusing.

"What do you mean me? Hold on, where's a mirror, you need to take a good look at yourself." Den then pulled a face like a petrified child. "Have we got to go, but I want to do one more trick? Oh my God we're being chased, I think I just wet myself."

"I don't think so, I think you'll find you were the one wearing the brown trousers."

"Yeah right, whatever. Anyway let's get this over and done with."

They were sitting in Jack's car, an old Ford Capri. They'd parked outside a rundown jewellers in the East End of London. When they got out of the car, Jack slammed the door shut. It was cold outside and it had started to snow. Thick snowflakes blew in their faces, impairing their vision and forcing them to squint and pull the collars of their thick jackets tight against their faces. On entering the shop they were greeted by a small, balding man with a big nose and prominent nasal hair. So prominent, in fact, it looked like a long haired rabbit had tried to hide itself in his head and during the process got stuck in his nose.

"Back so soon gentlemen?"

"It's been busy Jerome."

"Ha," he scoffed, "I'm glad someone's doing well. It's been very hot around here lately, if you get my meaning, 'innit." Jerome had a peculiar accent: a mix between the Middle East and the East End.

"Come," he said while lifting up the wooden board of the counter. He then gestured to Den and Jack to go through into the back room.

"Now what have you got for me, gentlemen?"

Jack was wearing a thick, long oversized grey coat, which made him look like a Russian soldier from World War II. It had a large inside pocket. He reached in, pulled out a scruffy satin bag and placed it on the centre of the small circular table.

"My, my gentlemen, we have been busy, busy bees," Jerome said in a very sinister and deliberate way. He made Den feel uneasy. It was a sensation that grew stronger after Jerome placed a small round magnifying glass in his right eye and began examining each piece of jewellery. Den cringed as Jerome touched the clean bright surface of a gold necklace with his clammy, grubby hands.

After carefully examining each piece of jewellery he placed the treasure into five different piles. Den, who had the attention span of a sparrow, had already started looking round the room. He soon figured out that this was the most likely place that Jerome would keep his stock.

"Don't get any ideas, gentlemen," Jerome said without lifting his head or moving his eyes away from the task in hand. "My employer can be less than friendly if he catches anyone. The last person who so much as conspired to steal from him is very much regretting his decision."

"You got me all wrong there Jerome," Den replied casually. "After all if I stole from you, where would I fence the gear?" Although Den was trying to make light of the situation, he inadvertently gave away their bargaining position. There was another long pause as they waited for Jerome to make his assessment.

"Have you ever heard of David Blaine, Jerome?" Jack asked, breaking the silence.

"Not now," interrupted Den, putting his hand up. Jerome ignored them both and remained crouched over the jewellery, studiously carrying out his work. When all the chains had been separated into their different piles, Jerome pulled out a large calculator from the top draw of the battered old wooden desk that was in the corner of the room and started taping away.

"One and a half G's," he said coldly looking at Den.

"Nice one Jerome. Come on now tell us the real price."

"That is the real price," he replied removing the magnifying piece from his eye.

"You're joking right, for starters that's less than a tenth of what that's worth," argued Den. "Even I know the price of gold has gone up."

"Take or leave it. There's a lot of pressure at the moment. The police are cracking down on our little industry. The price reflects the level of risk. Everyone's getting squeezed," he said taking a long gulp out of the can of drink that was on the table. He then attempted to crush it in his hand but failed to make much of an impression.

"One moment, I need a word with my colleague," Den said. Jack didn't move from the chair, he sat there with a blank expression on his face.

"Oi that's you" Den said, stopping himself from being abusive. As soon as Jack got to his feet, Den put his arm round his broad shoulders and led him into the corner of the room.

"What do you reckon?" he whispered.

"We're stuffed. He's got us over a barrel. Don't know anyone else who could shift this much gear at such short notice. We could sit on it, but we both need the dough."

"Ok, but I really don't need this hassle any more."

"What if we try and negotiate?" Jack suggested.

"Not a bad idea, not a bad idea at all. Ok I'll give it my best shot," Den said breaking away from Jack and turning round to face the small, rotund frame of Jerome.

"Right Jerome, we can't do it for less than two and a half G's."

"One five, fifty."

"Two three."

"One six, that's my final offer."

"Deal," interrupted Jack.

"Hold up," Den said through gritted teeth, "this isn't the TV Jack; we're not watching Noel Edmonds." But before Den could argue any more, Jack shook hands with Jerome.

"I'll get the money," said Jerome keen to clinch the deal.

"What did I tell you? I'll do the talking. I'll give you deal or stupid no deal." But whatever Den said, it wasn't going to wipe the inane smile of pleasure off Jack's face.

*

Den pulled the top of his brown leather jacket together to guard against the cold. In his other hand he held a yellow betting slip. He took one last, long look at it before taking a few steps and throwing it in a bin. The idea had been a decent one: to win enough money to send Yvonne, Kevin and Freddie on holiday. She'd never been abroad, neither had he for that matter. But she'd read this story in a magazine once about going to a place in Italy, which was full of olive groves and orange trees. She always said it was like going back in time. When they were first married she'd attached a picture of this villa to the fridge with some magnets. Not every day, but probably once a week, Yvonne would smile and say that they would all go there some day.

Well it wouldn't be for a while now, thought Den, who'd managed to turn the £800 that he'd started the day with into £8. It was the last time he was ever going to take a tip from Jack. He waited for a lorry to pass by and then crossed the road. The air was crisp and dry. Den sauntered along stopping to kick a stone. After several hits he eventually knocked it into a lump of snow. As he walked, the houses began to disappear and were gradually replaced by trees. Then the headstones came into view. Their distinctive shape made Den feel alone and isolated, even in the day time. The weather was getting oppressive: an overcast wintry day that had an unsettled edge to it. Patches of snow were on the ground. It was all that remained of the flurry earlier in the day. Den turned left up the pathway and then weaved his way through the graves before finding an area where there was a series of placards, either on the ground or attached to arches and wooden frames. In the distance he saw a hearse parked up by the main building of the crematorium. He stopped and stared at one of the plaques.

GREGORY JOHNSTON

BORN 26th July 1946

DIED 24th December 1992

May his soul rest in peace

"You won't believe how much Freddie looks like you. He's got your eyes and your ears and nose. It's mad, I'm telling you." Den paused for a moment and then studied a nearby bench, which looked too damp to sit on. He walked up to it, pulled out a plastic bag from his coat pocket and carefully spread it out, before gingerly sitting down. He leant forward, resting his forearms on his knees, his hands clenched together.

"Do you remember that time we went ice skating? It was a long time ago. You made me laugh because at one point you were out of control and ended up knocking over that big couple. You said it was lucky because the woman broke your fall," Den said smiling to himself. He had another quick look round to make sure no one was in earshot of his conversation.

"I only say it because I went with the kids and Yvonne, yesterday." There was a pause as Den became thoughtful. He reached into his jacket pocket and pulled out a miniature bottle of Bell's whiskey. He got up and placed it beside the plaque.

"Anyway, happy birthday dad. Don't worry; it's your favourite, Bells. I know I shouldn't encourage you. But it can't do you much harm now."

"You did have a temper on you though, didn't you? Remember that time that man in our local, the Frog and Radiator, wouldn't serve you. What did he say again? 'There's more chance of seeing a flying pig than there is of me serving you', and then he laughed at you. You went ballistic. I've never seen anyone go through the air like that. What was it you said? 'Fly piggy fly, oink, oink'. You certainly could throw a punch for a little guy. Never going to forget that." Den winced as he recalled the punches and the kicks and the bruises he'd sustained over the years.

"Still, can't really judge you anymore can I? Made a right pig's ear, get it, pig's ear of my own life. Yvonne's kicked me out, haven't got a penny to rub together. What a joke I turned out to be. Look at that…" Den said holding out his shaking hand, "…can't even tie my own shoelaces some days. Like father like son."

"Wonder what advice you'd give me, you know, if you were still here and you'd cleaned your own act up. Perhaps, perhaps, one day you'll forgive me for what happened." Den held his head in his hands.

"God I miss you. I really really miss you. If ever I needed some help, it was now. If ever I needed someone to talk to…"

*

It wasn't unbearably cold but it was the kind of temperature that, after a while, seeps into your bones to give you a chill that is hard to ignore. By this point Den didn't have much feeling left in his toes. The thought of going back to his bedsit and spending another night making dinner and watching reality TV on his second hand telly with a crackly reception, wasn't that appealing. As he rounded the corner, the local pub came into view. He breathed in through his nose and, with a peculiar heightened sense, could make out a faint smell of beer which was lingering in the air.

He was feeling low and was in the sort of frame of mind where he was questioning everything. The bad decisions that he'd made and the times he'd let people down, especially those closest to him. In fact, what was the point to his life if his only comfort was a drink, and this was the one thing he was denying himself?

The group, his support group, had given him a list of numbers to call in an emergency, or as he liked to think of it, in a moment of weakness. Well this was one such occasion but as lady luck would have it, he'd left the numbers in his other jacket. He quickly checked all his pockets, just in case, but he was pretty sure that's where it was. He checked his mobile phone and realised he had no calling credit left. It would have been a short conversation.

Today was a special day for Den. It was his dad's birthday and rather than remember the way he died, which was an experience he didn't want to revisit, Den wanted to remember the way he lived. So although it might have seemed weird to some people, he liked to celebrate it in the way that his old man would have appreciated. A toast to his dad, God rest his soul. The trouble was that, in the past, most of his toasts had blurred into one long toast.

Despite the moral dilemma Den was facing, he found himself being drawn towards the pub, as if it had cast a magical spell over him. The pub pied piper playing his favourite tune. And then the debate started in his head. What harm would one drink do? He'd been good, so good in fact, that it wasn't a problem anymore. But what would Yvonne think? Well she never believed him in the first place. Perhaps she was right. Then there was Freddie and Kevin. They'd noticed the difference, they'd told him so. They didn't have to know though. After all it was a quick glass of whiskey to remember his dad. He needed to go somewhere where there were people, for the company. Perhaps have a quick go on the fruit machine, grab a packet of crisps or even some chicken and chips in a basket. After all he had £8 plus his dole money.

He paused at the door and was forced to take a side step as two men, dressed in jeans and heavy coats braced themselves against the rush of cold air. They were talking about football as they made their way towards the car park round the side. He stood there, staring at them, but their complete lack of awareness of him made Den feel insignificant. He turned away and took three, maybe four steps but in a moment of indecision turned back and forth and back again before finally walking in through the door. As he pushed it open, he was greeted by the noise; it was so instant it was almost like switching on a radio which had the volume preset at a high level. It gave him an overwhelming sense of belonging. Home to him was a crowded, dark pub full of drinkers smelling of beer, with TV screens showing football matches, people crowded round pool tables or putting coins in the slots of fruit machines, wooden chairs and rows of optics. Not everyone's idea of heaven, admittedly, but to Den at this moment in his life, it was his.

"What can I get you?" asked the barman, while he was wiping the bar top with a cloth.

"What?"

"Well this is a pub mate; generally people come here to have a drink?" he said, and then laughed while looking at one of the many stooges, gathered around the bar.

"Give me a minute will you?" Den said feeling disorientated, as if he'd been asked to recall some complicated numerical algorithm.

"Suit yourself."

Den grabbed hold of the nearest bar stool and gently lowered himself onto it. It was like he was hungry for a drink, not just thirsty. More like a craving driven by an addiction but at the same time he was aware that no good would come of it. Like an addict, it was often the pain which brought pleasure. It was the burning sensation at the back of his throat which gave him a sense of comfort. Self-punishment: the fulfillment of an act of self-loathing. Quenching the hate inside, the insecurities that had been spawned by an unstable childhood and a life of misadventure. Then it suddenly came to him, why he was there, sitting in a dark pub on a cold and wintry night. He leant forward with his hands on the bar, staring at the barman.

"I'll have a double Bell's whiskey," he finally said, licking his lips.

Part Three
Tom and Den

Chapter 1
New Year's Eve - seven hours in prison

"So are you feeling lucky Tomski?" Duncan asked, waiting for a reply. When none was forthcoming he leant forward and began shouting in Tom's ear. "I said, are you…"

"I heard what you said. I don't respond to Tomski."

"Ok, what about Tom?"

"Well I don't really fancy anyone in here to be honest," and then Tom thought he might tell Duncan about Angela, the girl that he met ice skating but when he saw Rick heading towards them he decided against it.

"Alright ladies," said Rick, who'd come from the direction of the toilets, looking pleased with himself. He casually strolled up to them and then gently slapped Tom on the back.

"Don't you start," replied Tom.

"What? Come on Tom cheer up, I'm celebrating. So do we all fancy a bit of bubbly or what?"

"What are we celebrating?" asked Tom. Duncan and Rick gave

each other an awkward glance.

"The New Year, Tomski," said Rick. "Don't you remember? Quite common apparently, that this is a day of celebration. Better times ahead and all that." Rick's bluntness made Tom feel stupid. On top of that he didn't fancy drinking champagne tonight. Having said all that, he didn't want to appear ungrateful.

"I guess I can force a bit of bubbly down my throat if you're paying, Rickski."

"That's the spirit," replied Rick.

Rick had managed to secure their usual half moon table, which given the occasion was an impressive feat. So Tom made himself comfortable while Rick and Duncan went to the bar to get the champagne.

Bar Enema was heaving for the New Year's Eve party as people queued three deep at the bar. As he sat there, Tom's mind began to wander. It was finally dawning on him that his relationship with Chloe was over and he had no choice but to move on. In fact his whole life was in need of major restructuring and he was waking up to the fact that he was the only one that could do anything about it. Looking on the bright side though, it couldn't get much worse. He'd lost the woman he adored, the business that he loved and the relationship with his granddad that he cherished so dearly. What better way to herald in a New Year than with a new plan for a new life, to take a new direction and become the person he'd always wanted to be. The slight flaw to it all was that he had no idea which way to go. His eyes moved round the room full of party goers, any one of which looked like they knew exactly where they were heading: high-flyers that appeared to have plenty of friends, money and purpose in their lives.

As Tom sat there staring in the general direction of Rick and Duncan, he went into a trance like state. Suddenly he was snapped out if it by the sound of an incoming text message. He reached for his jacket, which was on the seat next to him, and fumbled through the pockets until he found his phone. There was no message. Curiosity got the better of him and he quickly began to check the other jackets for phones, starting with Rick's. When he pulled Rick's phone out of the inside pocket, he discovered that it had just received a message. He looked up to see where they were and eventually spotted them standing at the crowded bar. He then did what he felt was the respectful thing and put Rick's mobile phone back into his jacket pocket. Tom sat there for a few restless moments.

He couldn't explain it but something beyond normal inquisitiveness got the better of him. He'd developed a nagging desire to see who'd texted Rick. After looking up one more time, to check the location of his friends, Tom pulled out Rick's phone and casually held it under the table. He then flipped it open.

> 1 message received
> I wish we could be
> together tonight but
> then weve got a
> lifetime of special
> moments am so glad
> you asked me to
> marry you I miss you
> xxxxxxxxxxxxxxxxxx

Tom counted at least ten kisses. That explains why he wants to celebrate, he thought. He knew there was something more to it than New Year's Eve. Rick must have wanted to keep it a surprise. Before he had time to check who'd sent the message, Duncan was on his way over with the first bottle of champagne. Tom quickly placed Rick's mobile phone back where he found it. Rick soon followed with no less than five ice cold champagne glasses.

"I got a few extra glasses in case any deserving ladies might want to join us, if you get my drift," Rick explained carefully placing each of them on the table. He then proceeded to pour out the bubbly yellow liquid and was about to propose a toast, when Tom interrupted.

"If you don't mind Rick," Tom said, getting up from his seat and then ushering him quiet with a hand gesture. "I'd like to take this opportunity to say a few words." He didn't give Duncan and Rick any time to complain. "I must admit that I always thought you'd be the last to go, to be fair, and I guess she must be one special lady but, and I think that I speak for all of us when I say, congratulations on getting hitched."

Duncan spat the contents of his mouth out over a couple who were engrossed in a conversation on the table next to them. Rick nearly spilt his drink down his shirt and spent the next few minutes choking and banging his chest with the palm of his hand.

"How did you know about that?" Duncan eventually managed to say.

"Let's just say that you can fool some of the people some of the time, ehh, you dark horse Ricky boy."

"What, and you're ok with it?" said Duncan in disbelief.

"Yes, of course I am. A bit surprised but yeah I'm cool." At this point Rick stood back and tried to signal to Duncan not to say anything else, but his friend wasn't looking.

"What, you're ok that Rick's marrying your ex-girlfriend who you've been obsessing over for the last year?" Duncan said, almost laughing in relief.

"He's what?"

"Errh, nothing."

"Did you? Are you?" but Tom didn't say much after that, he was too busy trying to smash Rick's head through the wooden half moon table.

*

The acrid sweet taste of the dark liquid stung the back of Den's throat, but the pain was soon nullified by the wet, semi-fizzy bitter flavour of the mouthful of beer which followed it.

"See I told you you'd feel better for a few drinks," explained Jack, slapping Den on his back.

"You know, for once I think you've got yourself a very good point there cuz." There was a pause in the conversation while both of them took several large gulps of the dark brown liquid, before taking a slower sip of their whiskeys.

"I hope you didn't put money on that old nag I told you about by the way," Jack said laughing. "What a donkey that one turned out to be. Was it last or second to last? It was all a bit of a mix up really. You know Ron from the butchers, he gets his hands on some lovely cuts of meat by the way, if you're interested. Had a nice bit of steak from there last week, very tender it was. Well he gave us the tip. Tells me the name of the horse was Ulysses but me being me only goes and writes it down as Lunas don't I, and when I looked in the paper just to check of course there wasn't a horse called Lunas but there was one called Luka…"

Den held his hand up like he does when he can't bear it anymore. Rather than getting angry, however, he looked at Jack and with a smile on his face said, "Get the next one in will you, Mr Blaine, and then you can show me that trick you do with the matches."

"Really, I thought you hated my tricks."

"Let's just say I've caught a bit of the old New Year's spirit," Den said passing Jack his empty whiskey glass.

"Ron said there was another cert in the 3:10 at Chepstow in a couple of days time."

"Would you be so kind as to get the drinks in, otherwise my mood is liable to change." Jack duly did what he was told and pushed his way through the horde of people at the bar to get two more pints of bitter and two whiskey chasers. In the meantime Den sat and attempted to savour his drunken haze. The trouble was any enjoyment was short-lived. A man stumbled and fell onto the table that Den was sitting at, knocking over his drink. The culprit was thick set, with tattoos all over his arms and in possession of a large beer belly. He said nothing, ignoring Den as if he didn't exist. Den stood up quickly to avoid being soaked by his own half filled glass of beer, as its contents spilled over the table and onto the stained pub carpet.

"A sorry wouldn't go amiss," Den shouted out to make sure he could be heard over the noise of the music. He spoke to the back of the man's bald head, which had red blotches on it from where it had been recently shaved. His right ear was pierced with a thick, gold earring.

When the man didn't respond Den went up to him and tapped him on the shoulder, first with his finger, then with his hand and finally almost punching him with his fist. It felt like he was hitting a brick wall. Eventually, like someone who'd been trying to ignore a fly, the type that buzzes loudly round your ears, the man slowly turned round to address the source of his irritation.

"What's your problem?" the man shouted, slurring his words. Den could now see his face clearly, the tattoo of a spider's web spread across the side of his thick neck. His big nostrils were gaping wide open, like uninviting caves. His thick, bushy eyebrows seemed out of place against the barren expanse of his forehead. The scar over his right eye looked like someone had tried to slice open his head. None of it was enough to intimidate Den. All he could imagine was how appropriate a matching one over his left eye would be.

Den was solidly built, but when he stood next to the man their height difference, to any outsider, made the contest appear one-sided. Den, all too aware of his physical disadvantage, spent time checking his opponent for a possible weakness. However hard he tried, Den couldn't get away from the fact that he was his father's son. The man who launched a barman through the air when Den was a little boy, was alive and kicking inside of him.

"You spilt my drink," Den said trying to control his anger.

"What are you going to do about it?" the bald man said with a hint of a West Country accent. Den shook his head and made a tutting noise.

"Now that's not exactly in the New Year's spirit, is it? Ok, I tell you what, why don't we forget about this little, misunderstanding and you let me buy you a drink?" The shaven-headed man didn't know what to say at first. It was like he'd been out-witted. "But you'll have to allow me to amuse myself by guessing what sort of drink you'd like." The man went to say something but Den wasn't about to give up the initiative. He held up his hand like he does. "No, no, don't spoil the fun." He then turned away and out of nowhere, with the swiftness of a martial arts expert, landed a punch on the side of the man's head, right on his temple. The bald headed man tried to hold it together but clearly looked dazed and ended up collapsing to his knees, like a wild buffalo that had been shot in the head. Den grabbed his earring and viciously pulled it, ripping the man's earlobe. Blood started pouring from the open wound.

"A bloody Mary, yeah I reckon that's your favourite drink," Den said before punching him square in the face. The man was defenceless, unable to react.

"Den, Den," came a voice from over his shoulder. He looked up to see Jack pointing to his right. When he turned round, he spotted a group of rough looking men who were heading in his direction. Rather than stand his ground, even Den knew when it was time to quit and began searching for the nearest exit.

That was when the police arrived unexpectedly, grabbing Den from what seemed like every direction. Pulling his hands behind his back and then slapping on the handcuffs, before he could break free. Jack tried to bargain with them but backed off after they threatened to cuff him too. Den was unceremoniously dragged out of the pub in front of an ambivalent crowd and shoved into the back of a police van, along with dozens of other party goers who'd been misbehaving. Happy New Year, Den thought as the policeman slammed the door of the van shut.

*

So far they'd stopped three times since Tom had, rather aggressively in his view, been thrown on board. Each time had led to an increase in the number of badly bruised men loaded on board, until it felt like being in a barrel full of bad apples. Tom hadn't bothered to plead his innocence. It came as a strange relief to be dragged away. It meant he didn't have to be anywhere near the perpetrators of his downfall. To be fair, the police had been quite reasonable but Tom had been in no mood to be reasoned with. His ex-best friend had got engaged to his ex-girlfriend behind his back and his other now ex-friend, Duncan, had known all about it. It was hard to imagine it getting much worse than that, but then he was stuck in the back of a police van on New Year's Eve, in desperate need of a toilet. His only wish had been that Rick had stood up long enough for him to land a proper punch, instead of the girl slap that he'd given him, while holding his head on the table.

After two more bodies had been pushed on board, a now familiar bang on the side of the van signalled that they were off again. Everything on the inside of the van seemed cold and hard and sharp. It meant that whenever they went round a corner or stopped abruptly—which it seemed was the only way the policeman knew how to drive—another part of Tom's soft anatomy incurred a bruise.

The people in the van were a mish-mash of men across all spectrums of London society. The one common thread which unified them was their drunkenness. Although Tom was immune by this stage, it must have smelt like a brewery in the back of the van when they eventually stopped and the constable swung open the back door. They were asked to file out in an orderly fashion, into the cold and uninviting night air.

When he got inside, Tom found the police station was packed with people who, given their varying degrees of inebriation, made it feel like a pub at closing time. The police officer behind the counter was in a jovial mood as she asked each person to empty their pockets and give her their personal details.

"Busy night Frank," she said. She was pretty in a manly sort of way: with short brown hair and no make-up.

"Could have done twice as many to be honest, just didn't have the room in the van," replied Frank, sounding bored.

"No chance you've run out of cells is there?" piped up one bright spark. He was a man in his late twenties, wearing a white T-shirt. It showed off the tattoos of snakes which ran all the way down his arms to the tops of his hands.

"As it happens, we have had a bit of a rush on," teased Frank, "but unfortunately for you it means that you're going to have to share."

"Come on give us a break?" said a rough looking skinhead, who nearly fell over as he stumbled up to the counter.

"Well if you're not careful I'll put you in with Marleen," smiled Frank, nodding his head towards a six-foot man wearing a pink jumper, tight leather trousers and black eye liner.

On hearing this Tom moved himself away from Marleen, as did several other people, probably the less drunk amongst the motley crowd. Frank then picked out Tom and led him into a room to take a statement. When they were finished, he took him back through to the main hallway and down a staircase into the depths of the police station. On opening the cell door, it was a relief for Tom to discover that he was going to share with what looked like a fairly normal man, who was already on the bottom bunk, fully stretched out with his hands stuck behind his head. Tom shuffled in like a lost sheep. The policeman then slammed the cell door shut behind him.

"Den's the name," Den said staying where he was but extending one hand from behind his head and offering it up to his new cell mate. Tom jumped at the gesture of friendship.

"Hi I'm Tom Kruise with a K."

"Well Tom Kruise with a K," Den said with more than a hint of sarcasm "welcome to my humble abode. It's not much but I like to call it home."

"Very nice" was all that Tom could think of saying.

"So what good deed did you perform to allow you to enjoy the surroundings of such a wonderful establishment?"

"It's a long story," Tom replied as he struggled to pull himself up onto the top bunk.

"That's alright. As luck would have it my 2am appointment can-celled on me at the last minute." Tom hesitated but he was so hacked off he felt like telling someone, so why not a total stranger.

"Well tonight my girlfriend, I found out my girlfriend, my ex-girlfriend, who left me a year ago, on Christmas Eve, in the afternoon, well more like the early evening. Well I found out she was, you know, had gone off with my best friend."

"Doesn't sound like much of a best friend to me," interrupted Den.

"Well he's not my best friend anymore," Tom said bitterly.

"Oohh what you going to do, hit him with your handbag," Den said inappropriately.

"Thanks for that."

"Oh come on Tom Kruise with a K, I'm only messing with you," Den said slurring his words a little. "These things happen. So your girlie has gone off with your best friend. What does that say about her and what does that say about you? She's the sort that will move on whenever she gets a better offer and you're the sort that knows the true meaning of love and friendship although, if I might be so bold, needs to improve the screening process when it comes to picking his friends. You, it would appear, have the moral high ground. A place from which you should be able to enjoy the view. There are plenty more fish in the sea, many of which will appreciate such qualities in a man."

"That's the sort of thing my granddad used to say," replied Tom.

"Well he's a wise man your gramps."

"Was, he was a wise man."

"I'm sorry to hear that," Den said, pulling himself up and sitting forward in his bunk. "So, if you don't mind, let me re-cap. Your girlfriend's run off, your gramps has passed on, to a much better place than this hell hole no doubt. Anything else? They say it comes in threes." Den's facial expression softened as he said this.

"My business, I own a chain of art galleries, with my business partner," Tom said hesitating.

"Carry on," Den said.

"Well it turns out that we've gone fifty grand into the red," Den let out a whistle just like Albert had, "and unless I can get the money soon, we're going to go bust."

"Bad break. So where did you meet this so called business partner? Friend of yours is he?"

"What Raymond?"

"That's right, the great Raymondo."

"At the squash club."

"Very nice, quick game of the old racquet ball, what-ho." Den said in his best posh accent. "And don't tell me, let me guess: he suggested that you use his team of people to set the whole thing up."

Tom was a bit surprised that this somewhat rundown, drunken, bloodshot eyed, stubble faced, untrustworthy looking man in the bunk below him could be so perceptive.

"That's right, he said we should use his accountant and his lawyer. How did you know that?"

"Not as stupid as I look," said Den smiling. "And, no don't tell me..." Den continued, putting his hands on his head as if he was a clairvoyant, "...he let you stump up the money, and then persuaded you to open up several more shops or galleries or whatever it was you said you did?"

"Art galleries."

"Yes that's right, art galleries. But then, further down the line, told you it had all gone pear-shaped."

"In a nutshell, yes" Tom said as he began to experience an increasing level of uneasiness.

"Well I'm afraid to say, Tom Kruise with a K, they saw you coming."

"What do you mean by that?" Tom said looking offended.

"Stitched you up like a kipper. You middle-class boys are sometimes the easiest of the lot I'm telling you. So trusting."

"Look, what are you saying?"

"Spelling it out to you in plain English, you've been conned, fleeced, taken to the cleaners, stung, whatever you want to call it. Used a version of it myself once as it goes," Den said while leaning back on his bunk bed. The stiff springs squeaked as soon as he changed position. "Not on such a grand scale of course. Mine was vegetables."

"Vegetables?" Tom said looking confused.

"It was lettuces actually. Always thought they were a veg. Anyway there was a shortage of lettuce right, bearing in mind this was, what, nearly twenty years ago so you didn't get the same amount of foreign stuff you get now. I managed to convince these two geezers to invest, well over four hundred pounds I think it was, which was a lot of money back then, to buy up all the lettuces in the local area. The idea being that we'd make a killing. Course I never bought any lettuces. Just phoned them to say that the market had suddenly been flooded with the things, we were running at a loss and that they owed me. Course I could be a bit more menacing back then and they nearly had kittens when they thought they had me on their case. Beautiful that was, the easiest four hundred quid I ever made. "How much did you put in, originally?"

"Fifteen," replied Tom looking sheepish.

"Fifteen hundred, that's a lot of dough."

"No, fifteen thousand."

"That, mate, is a serious amount of money. Sure beats mugging old ladies. But then the beauty of that scam was that every now and again you'd get someone who was stupid enough to go and get more money to try and save their business." Tom sat quietly on his bunk bed.

"Don't tell me you were thinking of doing that."

"No, no of course not." If Tom had looked down he would have seen a disapproving expression on Den's face.

"What can I do about it?" asked Tom.

"Well not pay him the fifty big ones for starters. It is illegal of course, so you could go to the police but then he's probably covered his tracks. You really need evidence. Receipts, a set of figures. Let me have a think about it."

There was a period of silence, as both lay quietly on their bunk beds in the damp and dreary cell, on uncomfortably hard mattresses, listening to the bangs and shouts from the other inmates. For the first time since he'd entered the cell Tom was starting to feel the cold, curling up to try and stay warm.

"What about you?" asked Tom.

"What about me?"

"Why are you here?"

"Oh, I lost my temper didn't I." Tom went quiet again. Sharing a cell with someone who'd just committed GBH never did feature in his top ten things to do before he died. Swimming with dolphins had recently come in at number nine but, unsurprisingly, being locked up with a thug hadn't made it in.

"Don't worry," said Den, "I know what you're thinking. You have to give me a good reason before I lose my temper."

"So what did the other person do?" Tom said in the most matter of fact way he could muster.

"Spilt my drink didn't he, the idiot."

"Oh," Tom said, making a noise that would have made a church mouse with cotton pads on its feet seem loud and inconsiderate.

"I'm pissed off with myself to be honest."

"Really," replied Tom, sensing his cellmate might be feeling remorseful of his actions and was taking the first steps towards a new, more responsible life.

"I haven't had a drink for what, over three months now and I was doing well, for once in my life, not that my life has been much to write home about."

"What, worse than mine?"

"That depends," said Den laughing ironically, "if you're divorced, living in a bedsit in Lewisham without a penny to rub together; no proper job and no future. Not exactly a roaring success. I've gambled away what little money I've ever had and only yesterday lost the money that was going to allow me to do the one decent thing I've done in my life, which was to send my family on holiday."

"We're a right pair aren't we?"

"Yeah we're a right pair of losers."

"Do you still love her, your ex-wife?"

"Yes, yes I do. Just don't know how to make it up to her. We're always arguing, well more like screaming at each other."

"Any kids?"

"Two boys, Kevin and Freddie. Kevin's the oldest, nearly twelve now."

"Imagine that, I can barely look after myself, let alone two teenage boys."

"Can't say I've done much in helping to bring them up."

"At least you're there now. What was it that someone once said to me. Everyday can be the first day of your new life or was it today can be the first day of your new life. Anyway you get my drift."

"Suppose you're right, got to leave the old Dennis Johnston behind."

"So what, were you out celebrating the New Year?"

"No not really, it was my dad's birthday."

"Oh ok, where was he then?"

"Six feet under."

"I haven't been there, is that one of those new theme bars?"

"No I mean he's dead."

"Oh I'm sorry, I didn't…"

"No, don't worry about it. It was a long time ago."

"How did, what did he die of?" Den went quiet, he was now lying on his side. He started nervously rubbing the back of his head.

"I killed him" said Den sombrely. His remark came from out of the blue and left Tom in a state of shock. Den quickly got off the bottom bunk to look Tom in the face.

"Don't look so worried, I didn't do it on purpose. I just couldn't stand there and watch him give my sister another beating. I'd tried to stop him before, when I was a bit younger. Took a right pasting for it I can tell you. He started on mum one night, well it wasn't just any old night although it felt like it; it was Christmas Eve. Pushed her down onto the kitchen floor and then stood there, bent over, waiting with his fist clenched until she dropped her guard and then 'bam' hit her square on the nose, blood everywhere there was."

"She could handle it though, but my little sister, she was only thirteen. She never did anything wrong. I, I didn't mean to do it," Den said as if pleading his innocence. "It was an accident. I caught him underneath his chin. The old fool was so drunk he slipped over. Hit his head on the floor. Whack," Den almost shouted the last word. The sound of his voice echoed around the cell.

"At first I thought he'd passed out but then claret started pouring from his head. When I got up it was all over me, all over my hands," Den said looking at his hands, as if reliving the experience.

"What happened next?" asked Tom almost breathless at the story his cellmate was recalling.

"He'd sent my mum off to the bathroom to look at her nose. When she heard what happened she came running in. She was holding a flannel on her face, trying to stop the bleeding. My sister had seen it all. I grabbed hold of my mum but she just kept screaming and beating my chest with her fists. When she bent down she almost slipped over in his blood. She held his head in her arms, stroking his hair until the ambulance came."

"My God," exclaimed Tom.

"Never talked to me since. Wants nothing to do with me." When Den said this his face scrunched up as if he'd just eaten something with a bitter taste. "Not once, even when the courts said it wasn't my fault. Not a letter, nothing. Just goes to show."

"To show what?"

"You think you do the right thing. Try to protect the ones you love and you end up hurting them."

"You didn't do anything wrong."

"Didn't I? I took my dad away from my mum."

"Accidents happen."

"What would you know about accidents?" Den said getting frustrated.

Tom went silent. He'd struggled to talk about what happened with Chloe and Rick let alone a subject he hadn't mentioned to anyone in over twenty-five years.

"I said, what would you know about accidents," repeated Den, getting aggressive.

Tom didn't reply or even acknowledge his cellmate. Den stood up again and glared at Tom.

"You don't scare me," Tom said trying to hide the fact that he was made to feel quite anxious by Den's actions.

"I errh didn't mean, that wasn't what I meant."

"What raising your voice and glaring at me?"

"I didn't raise my voice."

"Trust me when I say you can be intimidating."

"I, I, really didn't mean it. I guess I'm not used to telling anyone how I feel."

"I didn't ask you to tell me."

"No, no you're right, my mistake."

"It wasn't a mistake," Tom said, feeling bad that he might have upset Den.

"I thought you might understand," explained Den.

"I do understand, more than you think."

"How come?" Tom fell silent again. "Come on you can tell me."

"It's not like that."

"Like what?"

"It's nothing personal. I've never told anyone."

"What, not even your girlfriend?"

"No not even her."

"Don't you think it might help to talk?"

"Do you feel better?" Tom asked bluntly.

"In a way, yes."

"What kind of way?"

"It feels like a weight has been lifted from my mind. That in some way the burden has been shared: almost like a confession."

"Really."

"Yes really," Den said, with a much softer expression on his face. Tom cleared his throat and looked away. After a long pause, he finally started to recount his story.

"Each day, when I was a kid, I used to walk my little sister home after school. Jessica was her name. Jessy was her, was her nickname," Tom said struggling to say a name he hadn't uttered for such a long time. "She was lovely, the best little sister you could possibly wish to have. It was less than a mile, the distance we'd have to walk to get back home. We always stayed off the main roads; practiced the green cross code," Tom said half laughing but stopping abruptly.

"One day, it was a Thursday, I'd taken my football into school, to play with during the lunch break, and I had it under my left arm," Tom said gesturing with the relevant hand, and making his left arm bow shaped. "We were on a slight hill and, well, the ball slipped. It started rolling down the hill and then hit the lip of a manhole cover. The odds were it would have rolled under a parked car, or just stayed on the pavement, but it didn't. It bounced out into the road. Jessy being Jessy, the thoughtful type, ran out. I shouted out to her but I don't know if she ignored me or the wind took the sound of my voice away. I mean it wasn't like her not to stop, not to listen to what I might say, if you know what I mean. It was a young guy, still a teenager. Said he didn't have time; that she ran out in front of him. All I heard was the thud as she was hit. I'll never forget that sound. She didn't die straight away. They kept her in overnight, on a life support machine. Her body twitched as she lay there but I knew she was gone. They couldn't stop the bleeding you see, inside her head. Even if they could have operated, which they couldn't, but if they could chances are, she would have been, well would have been…"

"It's alright," Den said in an attempt to console his cellmate. "I know it's hard but you've got to try and accept that it was an accident, that it wasn't your fault.

"You just said that you blamed yourself, for what happened with your dad."

"I guess if I'm really honest, I'm coming round to the fact that I can't change the past. I mean what else can I do? I've tried drinking myself into oblivion," Den said lightening the sombre mood a little. They both sat there for a moment. Neither of them knew what to add to the conversation to make the other feel any better.

"Where's she buried?" asked Den.

"Blackheath cemetery."

"Same place as my dad. Do you go to visit very often?"

"I've tried, loads of times. Even when my granddad was cremated there I couldn't bring myself to visit her grave. Guess I'm a bit of a chicken."

"No mate, you're not a chicken. You're trying to deal with the guilt, of feeling responsible for losing your little sister. Nothing wrong with that," Den said putting his hand on Tom's shoulder, "nothing wrong with that at all."

Chapter 2
New Year's Day – eight Christmas hymns

Tom woke up to an unfamiliar sound. He wasn't sure but he thought it could have been something metal being dragged along the ground. He was in his bedroom, lying on his double bed, fully clothed, in semi-darkness. Everything was a shade of grey, as if the colour had been drained out of all four corners of the room. Light was coming in through the window produced by the glow of a full moon on a clear night. It was cold, so cold in fact that Tom could see his breath as he raised his upper body to sit up in bed. The noise was eerie and getting closer. He was starting to feel on edge. There was something not quite right about it, not human.

Then without warning the bedroom door flung open and standing there, like something out of a Dickens novel was Tom's mother— well an older version, perhaps by as much as twenty years. Her face, like everything else in the room, was grey. Her eyes were dull and sterile. Following close behind her was another ghostly figure. Tom soon recognised it to be Raymond, his business partner, dressed in a grey suit that had a retro style: big lapels and a square cut. Around his body was a thick metal chain. Positioned in the middle of his chest was a giant padlock, fixing the chains to his body. Finally a third figure appeared. It was Chloe, wearing a long flowing dress with rough edges. Unlike the others she was elevated above the floor and came floating into the room. They positioned themselves at the end of his bed.

"You must pay for what you have done," said the ghostly figure of Tom's mother.

"Pay for what, I haven't done anything," Tom replied nervously.

"Murderer," said Veronica, pointing a long, spindly, withered finger at Tom.

"Murderer, murderer, murderer," chanted the three ghosts.

"Where did all the money go?" shouted the ghost of Raymond. He then made a nasty, cackling noise.

"You stole the money, that's where it went, I'm onto you," Tom said, defiantly trying to fight them back with his words.

"Rick's ten times more of a man than you'll ever be," screeched the ghost of Chloe, as she hovered towards Tom over the end of the bed. It made him move back up against the headboard. When he couldn't go any further, he decided to jump out of bed and then, as they continued to creep towards him, he edged away, moving nearer and nearer the bedroom window.

"Ten times more of a man, ten times more of a man, ten times more of a man," the ghosts chanted in unison. His mother's ghost then pointed with her right hand towards the bedroom window of Tom's eighth storey flat. Suddenly the window flew open and a burst of freezing cold air flooded the room.

"Pay for what you did…where'd the money go…ten times more of a man," they chanted until it became a mish-mash of words whizzing around the room. They started to close in on him. His only escape was the window. He peered out but all he saw was blackness. He took one last look at the grotesque expressions on each of the ghosts' faces. He could see the black lines under their hollow eyes and their rotting teeth. Their stench as they came closer was almost unbearable. He covered his nose with his hand and then without further thought threw himself out of the open window. Falling, falling, falling…down, down, down…his arms and legs flaying in the air, like an insect that has been flipped on its back and can't get up again.

"Tom, Tom," said Den shaking his cell mate's arm. "Come on, they're letting us out."

"I'm not a murderer, I'm not a murderer," Tom said moving his head from side to side and flapping his arms around. Den had to pull his hand back to avoid getting hit.

"Come on, look lively you lot," shouted the policeman. Den helped Tom to his feet and they made their way, single file out of the cell, down the dark corridor and up the stairs they'd been led down the previous night. The policeman behind the reception desk, who was in his late forties, with not much hair left, gave them both a warm smile.

"Right, let me see, Kruise, Tom. What have we got here? Abusive behaviour," he said looking at the sheet in front of him. "You called the police officer a pinhead. Not very original now is it. Bet you've never heard that before, have you Keith?" The policeman standing at the far side of the station smiled back in acknowledgement. "The bouncers said they had to pull you off your friend and that you slapped him several times round the face."

"He wouldn't stay still long enough for me to punch him," replied Tom, demonstrating to everyone in the room that he still needed to engage his brain.

"Well I'm sure that you'll go far in a court of law if you take that attitude Mr Kruise. But, given Her Majesty's generosity over this Christmas time and due to the fact that no one wanted to press charges, you can consider yourself a very lucky man. Although I don't think your custom, at whatever the nightclub you were in, will be welcome in the future. So that's it, sign here, collect your stuff from the lovely Janice over there. It's what we in the trade call a 'slap on the wrist' and don't let me see your face in here again."

"No, errh, yes sir," replied Tom sheepishly.

"Right, next we have a Mr Johnston; Dennis Leslie Malcolm, disorderly conduct in the Dog and Duck, where in your own words, you were assaulted by 'a bald headed git with no manners'. So is that what you were trying to do Mr Johnston, teach him some manners?" the bald headed policeman said while he pulled out the sheet of paper from his clipboard, in order to study it more closely. Den had real trouble holding back a smile when he heard the policeman read out the words he'd written in his statement the night before.

"But as he was also less than helpful with our enquiries. In fact he refused to say much at all when we took a statement. The owners of the Dog and Duck weren't interested in pressing charges. So it would seem that Christmas has come early for you as well. Same thing, get your valuables and I never want to see you in here again."

"Happy New Year," said Den smiling.

"A Happy New Year to you too," replied the policeman raising his eyebrows in a fatherly way.

They both quickly collected their belongings and then made their way out of the police station. When they stepped outside they were greeted by a brilliantly light, and painfully bright, landscape. The sun had just started to rise, its rays dancing off the cacophony of white which surrounded them. The snow, which had fallen silently during the night, had settled to more than a foot deep and it could have only just stopped as there was almost no sign of a disturbance to break the white carpet which lay before them. It made the whole of Greenwich seem pure and idyllic. It was early in the morning on New Year's Day and it felt like they were the only people who weren't tucked up in their beds, trying to sleep off a hangover. The atmosphere was calm and serene. Both men sucked in the cold, crisp air and breathed it out slowly.

"Which way are you heading?" asked Den.

"That way," Tom said, pointing towards the river.

"Have you got a spare half an hour?"

"I'm ready for my bed to be honest," Tom replied with the best excuse that he could come up with.

"I promise I won't mug you," Den said with as honest a look as he could manage on such a cold winter's day.

"Oh no, I didn't think that you…"

"I know, I was only joking. I promise it won't take long," he said persisting.

"Where did you want to go?"

"I wanted to take you somewhere that might help you."

"Help me with what?"

"You know, your past. What happened when you were a kid."

Tom was lost for words. He was genuinely touched by Den's offer of help.

"Really?"

"I just want to show you something that might, I don't know, make a difference. But you're going to have to trust me."

"What, a criminal like you." Tom said joking.

"It takes one to know one. But yeah you got a point; make sure you hold onto your wallet. Come on we can cut through the park."

"Ok, but go easy on me. I'm feeling delicate."

They walked down the road from the police station, crossed over Croom's Hill, past the Spread Eagle restaurant and up Nevada Street until they reached the park gates. It was a rare and wonderful sight for both of them, seeing Greenwich Park covered in an almost perfect blanket of soft snow. Despite all of the serious problems both faced, they had time to appreciate this wonder of nature. The sun was climbing higher in the sky, its rays causing the snow to sparkle and glisten, as if it contained a million tiny diamonds. A lone blackbird squawked in the distance and flew to the tree closest to them as they were walking. It swooped down and landed awkwardly on the snow, moving its feet quickly, to avoid sinking too deeply. Its hopping motion left a trail of clear symmetrical marks.

"So what sort of things do you like to do?" Tom asked trying to make conversation.

"What do you mean?"

"I don't know, some people are so busy that they don't even have time to think about what it is that they really like to do. I mean what do you do, that you enjoy?"

"Well painting. I like to paint, it chills me right out and sends me off to another place. A happy place if you like."

"That's pretty good," commented Tom.

"Keeps me off the streets. You must like to paint, what with your professional interest?"

"Can't do it myself I'm afraid. I can appreciate the finer art. Got a well trained eye for it, at least I thought I did until my business started to do badly. Not much good when it comes to doing it myself."

"Is it a case of can't do it or you're worried what other people might think?" Den asked, half listening to the snow as it scrunched underneath his feet. Every now and again he had to check himself in case he lost his footing, his old trainers ill-equipped for such conditions.

"I think I've got some sort of a block, if I'm honest. I was great, apparently, as a kid, always came top of the class in art but now I only have to go near an easel and I get anxious. Not sure what it is really, just can't seem to get going."

"Painter's block," Den said thoughtfully.

"What about you?"

"What, blocks? Not really, I've had a bit of a gap. Twenty years. Hadn't picked a brush up since I was a teenager but I'm lucky, for me it's been like riding a bike."

"Can I have a look at your work sometime?"

"You can, but it's not that good."

"That's ok, you said you enjoyed it and that's all that counts really but you never know it might actually be worth something. You could be the next Turner or Constable waiting to be discovered."

"Get away. Wait till you see them, you won't think like that anymore and anyway haven't we had enough of constables for one day?"

"That's for sure."

They slowly made their way up the steep part of the park, towards Blackheath. When they reached the top, the excesses of the night before were starting to catch up with them and both were breathing heavily. The fresh air was holding off their hangovers but only just, and the lack of sleep was starting to weigh on their achy muscles.

"Which way?" Tom asked.

"Through here," replied Den as he led them towards one of the gates at the top of Greenwich Park. To get there, they cut through the flower gardens. As they walked Den admired the many ever-green trees that were dotted around. He remembered reading that they'd come from all over the world, from as far flung places as Canada. One looked like a hat that belonged to a giant wizard.

As they exited the park and began to cross the heath, the wind picked up. They could see where it had started to bank some of the snow. Every now and then a gust would catch them off guard, pass-ing right through them and making them shudder.

"I hope we get there soon," Tom said, "I'm not sure that I can feel my toes anymore."

Without him realising, Den was leading Tom towards Blackheath cemetery. All the time they were walking, it hadn't dawned on Tom what his new friend's intention was until they turned the corner and he could make out the tops of the gravestones.

"Are you taking me here?" asked Tom, looking pensive.

"I didn't sleep much last night, which given the circumstances, I'm sure you'll agree, was understandable and well, I got to thinking about you and your sister Jessica. You don't have to do this but I just thought that, well the thing that's helped me the most, you know, to come to terms with my loss, has been to visit my dad's grave."

Tom stopped walking and for a moment Den thought he was going to make a bolt for it or even have some sort of a screaming fit. Instead he just stood there and, like a child who'd lost their parents in the shopping centre, he looked vulnerable and afraid; uncertain of what to do next.

"I'm really not sure I can do this," Tom said, whilst struggling to breathe properly.

Normally Den wasn't one for pandering to people's issues; sympathy wasn't an emotion that he felt easily, if at all. Empathy even less so. But this was something different, a feeling that he could definitely relate to. The burning desire to want to run away from reality. To hide from ever visiting that place which would spark his emotions, which he'd locked away for so long, for so many years in the deepest, darkest corner of his subconscious.

"Look, I'm not saying it's going to be a breeze mate. It's going to be tough but, well, you can't run forever. Let's put it this way, your life, like my life, can't get much worse, right? I think we're both agreed on that. Your girlfriend's left you, your business partners fleeced you, blah, blah, blah."

"Thanks for reminding me. I feel a whole lot better now," said Tom bluntly. He was feeling so low he wondered if things would ever get any better.

"I didn't mean it in a bad way. It depends on which way you look at it. Rock bottom means that the only way is up."

"Yes, but how do you know that?"

"Well, if I'm honest, I don't know for sure. I can't stand in front of you and say with one hundred per cent certainty but what I can tell you is, if you do this, and trust me I know it takes guts, if you do this then you will be able to face up to any hardship in your life, no matter how tough. More than that, you'll be able to look at yourself in the mirror and be proud of who you are. If you face the demons from your past, then the road to happiness lies straight ahead of you."

Tom stared at Den, standing in front of him, looking tired and hung over, his close cropped hair, his brown leather jacket with its rough edges and he wondered. He wondered what he was doing standing outside a cemetery in the freezing cold at nine o'clock in the morning on New Year's Day with someone he'd only met the night before in a prison cell. Had his life got so bad that this was what it had come to?

But Den was right, what exactly did he have to lose apart from his sanity and he was beginning to believe that this had gone already. There was nothing more to be afraid of. There was literally nothing left to be taken away, that hadn't already gone. Part of him believed that perhaps he never deserved any happiness, after what he did when he was a child. All the time he was with Chloe he lived in trepidation, looking over his shoulder, wondering when she was going to come home, who she was with. Now he knew exactly where she was and his worst fear had materialised.

"Tom, come on mate, we can't stand out here forever. At least we can keep warm looking for her headstone," Den said beckoning to Tom with his hand.

"I don't know where she is," Tom said sounding worried.

"That's alright mate we can look together."

Tom pushed his hands deep into the pockets of his smart beige, designer jacket and started to make his way in between the snow covered gravestones. It took them a while to find what they were looking for. When they did, it proved to be very unassuming: just a plain stone cross with a silver plaque on the front.

"It's over here," Den called out. The news came as a surprise to Tom who'd almost given up; hoping in a way that they didn't find it. He quickly made his way over to where Den was squatting down, clearing the snow away. It was a lovely spot not far from a magnificent old oak tree. To the right were a set of rose bushes that had been cut back. Tom imagined how lovely they would look in the summer time. He lent over to read the plaque which Den had cleared.

Jessica Kruise
Born 5th October 1977
Died 18th December 1984
Sent to us from heaven
Taken away from us too soon

We will love you always and forever
May you rest in peace

"Now what," Tom said nervously.

"Well," replied Den, sounding unsure himself, "I, when I first came to visit my dad's grave I thought of a happy time, that we had together. You know a time when we really connected. Had a laugh."

Tom went quiet. He looked up at the tree which had snow precariously stacked up on its branches, some of it was as much as an inch thick. One small tap, or a strong gust of wind and it looked like it would all topple to the ground. A representation of the fragility of life.

"There were loads of times really, but I do remember one in particular. Jessy really loved, and when I say loved, I mean really loved, Christmas; everything about it. I'm not sure if it was because of our grandparents' influence or not. But for her, being happy meant long winter nights by the fire, shopping for presents, wrapping presents, the nativity, decorations, Christmas films."

"Well one Christmas Eve, I remember mum and dad took us into Blackheath Village, around late afternoon as it was getting dark, just before the shops shut. It was a complete surprise. Apparently they'd been planning it for ages. They got us a hot chocolate each which was a real treat. We stood there waiting at the bottom of the hill, round the corner from the train station with perhaps as many as a hundred other people. Jessy was constantly asking mum why we were there and mum just kept on saying 'be patient, you'll find out soon enough.' Then we heard music, very faint at first. It was a brass band. The wonderful sound of a trombone filled the night air with "Good King Wenceslas". Jessy's face was a picture, her eyes were wide open when the brass band came marching up the road. Behind them was Mary and Joseph, Joseph held onto the reins of a donkey that Mary was sitting on. Not the Mary and Joseph, obviously, but two teenagers from the village that had volunteered. Behind them was a whole crowd of people. Jessy got so excited that mum had to grab hold of her hand to stop her from running off. I was eight years old at the time. We then mingled in with the crowd. When we finished the short walk up to the church, the brass band stopped playing and positioned themselves on the steps. They'd put extra spot lights up nearby on the heath and lots of people were carrying lanterns. I mean it couldn't have been more Christmassy. A big crowd gathered and some people were carrying song sheets, with all the carols on them. Jessy would not, could not stop smiling. The vicar said a few words. I can't recall exactly what."

Tom stopped telling his story and at first Den thought he'd forgotten what he was going to say next but then he looked at his face, he realised that a tear had trickled down his cheek. Having gone through a similar experience at his AA meeting and realising that crying in front of strangers made him feel uncomfortable, Den tried to make Tom feel better.

"It's alright Tom."

"It's just that Jessica loved to sing. Not like me, I've always had one of those voices that dogs howl along to." Tom said half-smiling through his tears. "She had the voice of an angel. It was as if singing set her free. She was so full of life." Tom pulled out a handkerchief from his trouser pocket and blew heavily into it. He squatted down closer to the gravestone and ran his fingers over the plaque, following the engraving of her name as if spelling it out.

"Her favourite carol, out of all of them, was The Twelve Days of Christmas. We waited all evening before they sang it. Something like seven carols went by and my face had gone numb and my feet were like icicles. I'm sure Jessy's were the same but there was no way anyone was going home. When they finally started playing it, she jumped for joy and sang her heart out. 'I love this one, I love this one' she said clapping her hands. Grandma used to play it on the piano at home, get the whole family round even the ones like me that were tone deaf. We'd all sing a line each. Jessy always made sure she sang 'the five gold rings' and then we'd all sing 'and a partridge in a pear tree' together." Den knelt down next to Tom and put his hand on his shoulder.

"There's nothing wrong with having happy thoughts. How are you ever going to feel happy if you never think of happy things? The past is in the past mate, you can't change it. I know you'd like to but you can't. We all make mistakes you know. Everyone does, otherwise we wouldn't be here. You can't go back and change what happened with your sister but what you can do is something about the present, the here and now. Learn to forgive yourself mate. You weren't driving the car that killed her, you were being a good brother and walking her home."

"But I didn't protect her."

"You can't protect everyone, all of the time. You ask any parent that. You can only ever do so much, the best you can."

"I miss her so much," Tom said punching the snow and the ground with his fist. "There isn't a day that goes by that I don't wish that she was still here."

"I know. I understand exactly what you mean," Den then lent forwards and with his arms outstretched, grabbed Tom round the shoulders and hugged him. Tom fell forward, the knees of his smart trousers sinking into the snow.

"If you want it to be, this could be the first day of your new life," but Tom didn't say anything instead he pulled away from Den, put his hands up to his face and wept, and finally after a lifetime of numbness, his heart opened up to the pain which he'd been avoiding nearly all his life.

Chapter 3
2nd January – nine wasted years

For what felt like the first time in his life, despite getting drunk on New Year's Eve, Den was feeling good about himself. He'd helped a fellow human being, which was a break from a lifetime's habit of doing the exact opposite. He wasn't sure where his motives were coming from—if the conversations at his AA meetings were starting to sink in—or whether or not he was just getting in touch with the real Dennis Johnston. Perhaps he'd finally started to shed his old self, like peeling an onion, to get to his core. The person we are all capable of being if we choose to be: compassionate, thoughtful, respectful, generous, kind and considerate.

"Watch what you're doing, you idiot," shouted a cyclist, after Den had stepped out into the road without looking properly.

"Back at you turnip head," Den replied, lifting his head up in order to project his voice at the stranger only to receive what Den thought was the 'V' sign, but wasn't sure because the cyclist quickly put his hands back on the handle bar as he sped off round the corner.

They'd decided to meet up at a café by Blackheath train station. It wasn't particularly convenient for Den or Tom but Den quite fancied another walk through Greenwich Park. It had snowed some more in the night. As he began the climb up to the top, where the Greenwich Observatory was, Den's legs soon started to feel the strain. No-one witnessed his discomfort or words of discontent, however, as the Park was unusually quiet.

When he reached the top, the views of the River Thames and Canary Wharf were magnificent. Den, who was panting from the climb, took in a few deep breaths and stood admiring the horizon. The snow-topped buildings made him feel like he was somewhere else, somewhere totally different. Not that Den had been to many different places, but he'd often tried to imagine what it must be like to live in a town in Sweden or Russia during the winter. To his left was the majestic Greenwich Observatory. Its telescope, housed in the dome, trained relentlessly on the sky, detecting the tiniest of changes in the stars.

As Den stood and gazed into the distance, he did what he always seemed to do when something good happened to him, he started beating himself up. He began to think about all the terrible things he'd done. The nasty words he'd uttered in hate. What if he hadn't hit Yvonne that night nine years ago, given her a black eye, bruised ribs and a broken and bloody lip. That was a turning point, even though he didn't realise it at the time. Up until then she'd let him back. That time was different though. The gentle girl from Charlton turned into the tough talking woman he knew now. She locked him out. Threw all his stuff over the balcony. Six stories down. His clothes went everywhere. He banged on the door so hard that the neighbours called the police. Just like his father. That's what really hurt. That he'd spent most of his life hating his father, only to become the very person he once despised so much.

The sound of a boy shouting out to his friend as he ran down the hill with a snowball in his hand, snapped Den back into the present moment. He glanced at his watch and realised he needed to get a move on if he wasn't going to be late.

*

Tom didn't know why he was such a stickler for time, he just was. So if anyone said meet you at nine-ish it would spark a chain reaction that would lead to high levels of anxiety. When asked, he couldn't explain such behaviour and found it even harder to shake free from it.

He glanced at his watch, 8:59am and almost as the second hand of his watch hit the twelve he pushed open the door. It was a small but comfortable café, with a large counter ahead of him as he walked in, displaying a comprehensive array of cold meats, cheeses, quiches, falafels, pork pies, olives and sandwich fillings. There was a fridge, to the left of the door, which jutted out with various cans and bottles of drink. The seats and tables were quite tightly packed together. There was a doorway at the far end with one of those half doors which led to the kitchen. The walls were covered by two large blackboards which had, written in coloured marker pen, an extensive, neatly laid out, menu. There was a bewildering display of choices the core of which Tom worked out was based around a traditional English breakfast and sandwiches. Tom loved his full English and was salivating at the prospect of filling his empty belly, especially on such a cold wintry morning.

It had been an emotional couple of days. Tom was understandably angry at Rick. He'd contemplated revenge; endlessly mulling the possibilities over in his mind. The thought of hiring some unsavoury character: Ronny 'the hit man' Richards, to do his dirty work for him. If possible, pay a bit extra for him to shoot Rick in each leg first, then each shoulder before inflicting the final fatal shot to his head, right between the eyes. The hit man, once finished with Rick, would then turn his attention to Chloe who, by this point, would be crawling on the floor trying to hide by the side of the bed, screaming for mercy. But he'd soon switch from thoughts of revenge to feeling like he wanted to talk to Chloe and ask her if it was what she really wanted.

Whether there was any chance, however remote, of salvaging their relationship.

It was typical that the one girl that Rick hadn't had first refusal on, was the one that ended up running off with him anyway. The two friends closest to him wiped from his life in an instant. If life was a box of chocolates, then Tom felt that he'd picked the tough one that not only locked his jaw up but caused an allergic reaction that made him vomit incessantly.

"Could I have a full English please," he asked the sour faced waitress who looked worn out, like she'd been deprived of sleep and home comforts for weeks. Under more normal circumstances he might have felt some sympathy for her but today he had enough on his plate.

"Cooks not in today, we're only serving sandwiches."

"Right well I guess I'll have..." Tom said turning round to look at the blackboard behind him, "...toasted cheese and ham panini with mustard please."

"Comes with salad."

"That's fine."

"Anything to drink?"

"Cup of tea please, one sugar."

"Sugar's on the table," she said, before embarking on the laborious round trip to get a knife and fork wrapped in a napkin. On her return she slowly unwrapped the said items and placed them in front of him.

"Thank you," he said in as chirpy a manner he could conjure up given the circumstances.

Out of the blue Tom's mind began to unnerve him with paranoid thoughts. What if Den wasn't going to turn up? The possibility of his new found friendship crumbling away, along with the rest of his life. Tom was touched that anyone would make such an effort for him. Bringing up the past like that. It was his fault, he'd always accepted that. He should have held onto the football, should have been more alert to the dangers. If he'd been more assertive with Jessica, it would never have happened. He'd gone over it a thousand times in his mind.

What had hurt was that no one had ever asked him how he felt about it: the pain of losing his little sister, his best friend. It was a taboo subject for him. His mum had always made it quite clear where she stood on the matter. The shock of that day had stayed with him, imprinted in his physical being. Like the needle of an old record player stuck on a high pitched shrieking noise, which kept sounding out over and over in his head.

"In your own world there Tom?" said Den pulling up a chair opposite him.

"Hello there," Tom said pleased to see Den. "Yeah in my own little world."

"Good, well is there any chance that, now you're out of it, you can rustle up a full English for us and...", he then paused and began rubbing his chin, "...a new life, one where I'm someone famous who has the arduous task of picking from dozens of beautiful women to go on a date with tonight."

"The cooks off I'm afraid," apologised Tom.

"Whose idea was this then?"

"It was yours."

"Alright I know, just pulling your leg. You need to lighten up a bit."

"What exactly have I got to be happy about? My…" But before Tom could get into full flow, Den had put his hand up, flat in front of his face, halting him in his tracks. Tom was flabbergasted.

"Have you any idea how annoying that is?"

"What is?"

"Sticking your hand in my face just as I'm about to talk."

"I've never had any complaints and anyway, I'm doing us both a favour."

"Right, well, how many friends have you got?" Tom replied.

"How many have you got?" asked Den.

"This isn't a competition and anyway I asked first."

"Well, there's my cousin Jack."

"He doesn't count."

"What do you mean he doesn't count? Don't let him hear you say that."

"No, you know I didn't mean it like that, I meant that he's family. So he doesn't count in the friendship category."

"Ok well there's my mate, Frank."

"How do you know him?"

"We used to do odd jobs together."

"Have you ever stuck your hand up at him, when he was trying to talk."

"No," Den said looking at the menu behind Tom. "'Excuse me luv, any chance of a full English."

"Cooks off today," came the terse reply.

"I know, but I was just saying to my friend here that I'm sure that a multitalented lady such as yourself, could cook a mean breakfast." The cold expression on her face melted in an instance to be replaced by a coy grin.

"My husband, well ex-husband, he would always compliment me on my breakfasts. Said it was the nicest thing he'd ever had."

"What, you or the breakfast?"

"Oh I say. Oi Glad, we got a cheeky one in today," said the waitress to her work friend behind the counter.

"And may I say what a fool he was to ever let such a fine woman slip through his fingers. Now if you could possibly find a way to provide us hungry workers with the fuel that we need to help us on our way and face a cold and frosty morning, we would be eternally grateful."

"I suppose I could give it a go, just this once."

"Thanking you kindly. Anyway Tom you were saying."

"I was about to tell you why I was unhappy."

"That's right," Den said sticking his hand up again.

"I am already familiar with your plight. Was there anything else, you know on top of what you've already said?"

"Isn't that enough to be getting on with?"

"Yes that is enough," said Den, who was in a reflective mood. "It's just that I've been thinking up a little scheme that could…"

"That could what?" Tom said eagerly.

"No you look like too much of a straight laced geezer to want to do something like that. No forget I mentioned it."

"Mentioned what, you haven't mentioned anything yet and what do you mean straight laced?"

"Ok let's put it this way. What's the craziest thing you've ever done, you know really mad."

"I've done loads of mad things," Tom replied shifting around awkwardly in his chair.

Den didn't say anything. He'd learnt from an early age not to fill in the gaps when someone was struggling. He waited patiently as the smell of burnt toast wafted over to them from the kitchen.

"I, well I, once I, I parachuted out of plane."

"Really?" Den said knowingly.

"Well, ok you got me there. I thought about doing it, once."

"I thought about jumping off the Empire State Building once. Don't count I'm afraid. Neither does having a friend of a friend down the pub who drove his motorbike through flaming hoops."

"I broke into my old school once," Tom said desperately trying to gain some semblance of credibility.

"Go on," encouraged Den.

"We all got drunk one night, myself and a few friends, and wondered what it would be like, you know, to see how our old school had changed."

"Did you get caught?"

"Well it was quite funny actually because we started messing around with the gas thingies in the chemistry lab and Josh did this trick where he filled his mouth with gas and then went to light it and nearly burnt his…"

"I didn't ask for your life history Tom, just whether or not you got caught."

"Yes, we did actually and we only managed to get off because the policeman on the case went on holiday the week before we were due in court and drowned in a freak boating accident."

"Lucky break. I suppose I could put it down to your lack of experience and a poor team. There is something there, I don't know. It's risky."

"What would be risky?"

"I'm probably going to regret this but we could break into, what's-his-names, your ex-business partner…"

"Raymond."

"That's it, old Raymondo's gaff."

"And do what exactly?"

"Well I told you I think it's an old scam. You may be shocked to hear this but my guess is he's stitched up loads of people. You weren't the first by the sounds of it and you probably won't be the last."

"No, it's too risky. He's got a safe and I don't know how we'd get the combination."

"Hold on, hold on, no one said anything about breaking into any safes and stealing things. Just a nose round to get some evidence. Didn't think you were that sort of a person?"

"I'm not, I'm not like that," Tom said defensively.

"You posh boys are all the same. It's ok to rob people of their hard earned pension money when you put on a fancy suit and sell them some dodgy insurance scheme but if someone steals a loaf of bread because they're hungry, then the law says you should stick them in jail and throw away the key."

"No one gets put in jail for stealing a loaf of bread anymore, what are you on about?

"Well that depends on who you know, if you know what I mean." From over Den's shoulder the waitress appeared holding two plates of what could have been anything. What was on the plates was so burnt, it was hard to make out.

"Here you go. I'm afraid that the gas is a little bit more powerful that I'm used to. So I hope you like it well done."

"Well done woman, it looks like you've gone and cremated mine," commented Den and then made the shape of the Holy Cross with his right hand. "God rest its soul."

"I knew I should have stuck with the cheese and ham sandwich," Tom said looking dejected.

"What are you complaining about, nothing like a bit of carbon to warm your body on a cold winter's day," Den said taking a bite out of a long object which he guessed was a sausage. He immediately spat it back out into his napkin.

"The only time carbon will warm you up is when you set light to it," Tom pointed out.

"To be honest I can now see why he left her."

"Who left who?"

"The waitress, never mind. Anyway are you up for it?"

"Up for what?"

"Christ do you ever listen? Having a snoop round old Raymondo's gaff."

"No, but I think I've got a better idea. Remember I told you my girlfriend…"

"Ex-girlfriend," Den corrected.

"That's right ex-girlfriend, well she still owes me some money."

"Remind me, how much was it again?"

"Fifteen."

"I'm not sure fifteen quid would make it worth our while to be honest."

"Fifteen thousand pounds."

"You need to be a bit more careful with your money, do you know that? Watch the pennies and the pounds look after themselves," Den said pushing his plate away.

"Alright O wise man."

"You can take the Michael all you want but I'm not sixty-five thousand pounds down."

"Anyway my ex-girlfriend, as you correctly pointed out, borrowed and I emphasise the word borrowed, fifteen grand."

"We could break into her flat and see if we can reclaim said borrowed item. Or, I have a suggestion if I might be so bold," said Den. "You could just ask her for the money back."

"Oh I tried that already."

"Let me guess, hold on," Den said putting his hand on his forehead as if he had some special psychic powers. "She told you to go back home and play with your Lego set."

"No, she said that she thought I'd given her the money."

"What and you didn't get her to sign an I.O.U. note? That's sloppy work there Tom."

"You've made your point," Tom said looking sheepish.

"It's alright, love is often blind," proclaimed Den.

"Yeah but not deaf and dumb as well."

"I'm not arguing with you. Ok I agree."

"Agree to what?"

"To help you recover, partially or otherwise, said lost money from your ex-girlfriend."

"Really."

"Yes, really."

"Ok well that's settled then."

"When?"

"Tomorrow ok with you?"

"No time like the near present," Den said. "Fancy a celebratory cup of tea?"

"Why not? At least she can't burn that," replied Tom.

"Good point," said Den gesturing to the waitress their order.

"What can I do, you know, to return the favour?" asked Tom.

"I haven't done anything yet."

"You took me to my sister's grave," Tom said, struggling to finish the sentence.

"No you're right, I did do that. Let me think. No, apart from helping me get back together with my ex-wife," he said flippantly.

"I can help you do that?"

"What, you think I should take advice from someone with your track record?"

"That's a bit harsh. Actually I'm too, I don't know, too giving, remember. The opposite of you. You could learn something from me."

"I can be giving."

"The only thing you probably gave your wife was a headache."

"Ok Casanova, give it your best shot."

"It's not as easy as that. Let me have a think."

There was a quiet moment, when all Den did was keep switching the salt and pepper pots around in one hand, his fingers moving intricately to displace one with the other and then back again. He kept doing this until the salt pot slipped through his fingers, spilling its contents on the table. For good luck or to avoid back luck, he then took a pinch of the spilt salt between his fingers and threw it over his shoulder, covering the back of the woman in the seat behind him, without her realising it. All the while Den was doing this, Tom was scribbling notes down on a half unfolded napkin. There was then the timely arrival of two cups of steaming hot tea.

"Right, ok, now this only works if you're honest, ok?"

"Ok Doctor Love."

"And if you're not sarcastic."

"Point taken."

"Have you ever said or done anything that you've regretted as far as your ex-wife is concerned?" Tom's rather naive comment made Den laugh, which wasn't the reaction that Tom had been expecting.

"The question you should be asking is, is there anything I've done right more like. You name it, I've done it. Got drunk, flirted with other women, hit her, got into fights, put her down, been angry, been rude." Den paused to take a sip of his tea. "So what's your point?"

"My point is, have you ever said you were sorry?"

"Sorry?" Den said as if it was some alien word from a distant galaxy. "I'm sure that, yeah I must have at some point."

"Remember, it doesn't count if you say it in your head," Tom said pointing his index finger at his temple.

"There is a slim possibility, however, that I may not have done. So go on."

"Well, it's a long shot but I reckon if you were to actually tell her that you were sorry for all the things you did when you were together then, well then maybe, she might…"

"She might what?"

"Learn to trust you again. Although that won't happen overnight."

"What, say sorry for everything?"

"Well all the things you actually genuinely regret, which may mean you have to listen to some fairly harsh stuff about yourself, that's going to make you feel bad about what you've done and you're going to need to accept that you were wrong."

"Yeah, and?"

"And tell her that you're a different person now, to the one you were then. That you've changed. You've grown and realised the error of your ways."

"Hold your horses there, can I borrow your pen?"

"Yeah," Tom said without thinking.

"Right," said Den licking the end of it, "say that again."

"Look it's no good if you have to write it down, it needs to come from the heart."

"What did you say after 'I'm a different person'?"

"I said," Tom stopped talking and put his hand over the napkin that Den was about to write on, "it's no good writing it down, it's got to come from here," he said pointing at Den's chest.

"What, my stomach?"

"No, your heart."

"How the hell am I supposed to do that?" Den said getting frustrated.

"You need to get in touch with how you really feel."

"This is turning out to be a lot harder than I thought."

"Come on let's try some role play," suggested Tom. "I'll be Yvonne and you can be you. Are you ready?"

"Fire away, darlin'."

"Come on you need to take this seriously."

"What?"

"I bet you never called your wife darlin," said Tom.

"Yeah, when she was in the other room," Den said smiling.

"Ok, you've turned up at the flat unexpectedly to talk to her and she says, what are you doing here, you weren't supposed to come round until Wednesday?"

"She doesn't talk anything like that."

"Just get on with it."

"What, say that bit again."

"What are you doing here?"

"I've, I've come to errh, I don't really know."

"I've come to see you," prompted Tom.

"Oh yeah, I've come to see you."

"Do you want money, because if you do, you're wasting your time. I haven't got any."

"No I didn't come all the way over here to ask you for money, who do you think I am?"

"Is the wrong answer," Tom said shaking his head.

"Well what the hell are you talking about," Den said crossing his arms and turning to the side.

"It's a test. I'm just pushing your buttons to see how you'll react. Come on let's try it again."

"I don't want to try it again."

"Do you want to win your wife back?"

"Yes," Den said like a ten year old school boy who wanted his 'Top Trump' cards back after they'd been confiscated by his parents.

"Is that a yes I want her back?"

"That's a yes I want her back," Den said reluctantly.

"Right, so let's try again. Den what a nice surprise, have you come to see the kids?"

"Yes, I mean no."

"No what."

"No, I haven't come to see the kids." There was a pause, as Den sat fiddling furiously with the salt and pepper pots.

"No, I've come to see you," prompted Tom.

"Right, no I've come to see you."

"Why's that?"

"I've got something to tell you."

"Good going," Tom whispered, giving him the thumbs up.

"Can't it wait, I'm cooking the dinner."

"It's important."

"What's so important that it can't wait until I've fed the kids?"

"I need to tell you now."

"Ok," Tom said shaking his head.

"What now, what have I done wrong now."

"Well, I think it's just better if you tell her at the right moment, when she's not distracted. So she can give you her full attention."

"Well I want to tell her now. What's wrong with that?"

"Den, it's not always about you."

"But I thought that it was about me; me getting back with Yvonne?" Tom was running out of energy to keep up the fight.

"Yes but sometimes you need to be flexible and fit in with other peoples' plans and then they are more likely to do what you're asking them to do, which is a favour for you. In this instance, you're asking Yvonne to give up some of her time, ok?"

Tom's initial thought was to walk out but for whatever reason, whether it was stubbornness or born out of loyalty, he was determined to see this one through to the bitter end. So instead he ordered another cup of tea. It was going to be a long day.

*

Den pulled up outside Yvonne's council flat and switched off the engine of his van. He hadn't phoned and she wasn't expecting him. It was probably the first surprise visit, certainly the first sober one, he'd made since she kicked him out nine years ago. Time, it is one of the weirdest things, he thought. It goes so quickly you almost wonder if it's nature's way of some cruel joke. You end up wishing it away but when you want it the most, it runs out.

He looked at himself in the rear view mirror. He was clean shaven, wearing his smartest shirt, the one he'd got in the sales and his best trousers. He'd bought some chocolates from the petrol station.

Den stepped out of his van. The beeping noise when he locked it echoed around the parking area of the square block of flats. He adjusted the shirt under his jacket, acting as if it was the most uncomfortable piece of clothing he'd ever worn.

When he went into the lift, a familiar stench of old urine filled his nostrils, making him wince. He pressed the lift button with crossed fingers and then looked upwards for some divine inspiration. It worked and the lift juddered into action. The only trouble was it moved so slowly, Den wondered if it had enough energy to reach the top, giving him a few anxious moments as he waited for it to complete its journey.

"Nine years," he whispered to himself. "Nine wasted, miserable years. Where did it all go wrong?"

As the lift doors cranked open, he began to panic. What if Yvonne didn't give a damn about him anymore? But that didn't tally up with what Freddie and Kevin had told him.

"Stay calm," he said clutching the box of chocolates tightly in his left hand. He then realised he was daydreaming when, as he strolled out of the lift, the doors closed on him and almost crushed the box. As he went towards the door of number 21, Den yanked the collar of his shirt one last time.

"Here goes nothing," he said as he rang the doorbell. It seemed to take forever for Yvonne to come to the door. It was like waiting for the kettle to boil when you're gasping for a cup of tea, with nothing to distract you but the noise of the element heating up the water. Finally the sound of footsteps could be heard and the twisting of the latch being turned.

"Who the hell are you?" Den said as he quickly hid the chocolates behind his back.

"Never you mind, who are you?" the young man with spiky brown hair replied confidently, as if he owned the place. He then inadvertently flexed the muscles in his thick arms, which couldn't be missed due to the black sleeveless T-shirt he had on.

"I'm, I'm Yvonne's husband." The man looked him up and down, as if trying to work out the exact nature of Den's business.

"Not the Milk Tray man then?" the young man said smiling.

"Who is it Jeffery?" came the sound of Yvonne's voice.

"Never had you down as a Jeffery," Den said sniggering. "Rudolf or Rupert perhaps, but not Jeffery."

"Man here who claims to be your husband." In an instant Yvonne appeared at the door, her make-up half done, wearing her favourite red blouse and a tight, thigh length black skirt.

"Den, what are you doing here at this time of night?"

"I was in the neighbourhood and...," he started to say, trying to act as nonchalantly as he could while keeping the box of chocolates hidden behind his back.

"I didn't know that you're married," Jeffery said looking surprised.

"Is that what he told you? No, no we're divorced, I kicked him out ten years ago."

"Nine."

"What?"

"It was nine years ago," confirmed Den, who was tempted to shove the box of chocolates into Jeffrey's hand and say 'Happy Anniversary' before punching his lights out. The red mist was beginning to descend but before it could consume him, it was replaced by a much deeper, over-riding emotion: one of hurt.

"Look it's freezing, I'm going to go inside. Nice to meet you, Yvonne's ex-husband."

"Cheers Jeff-rey."

"So what do I owe this unexpected pleasure?"

"Oh nothing. It doesn't matter," Den said backing away from the door.

"Are you alright?" Yvonne said looking him up and down with a quizzical frown on her face.

"Fine, fine, look must have got the time wrong. Thought I was seeing the boys, my mistake, see you Thursday.

"Today is Thursday."

"Did I say Thursday? I meant Friday. Oh is that the time, must be off, bye. Love to the kids."

Den turned on his toes and more by luck than judgment managed to hide the chocolates from Yvonne's line of sight. When he got to the bottom of the stairs, he went to one of the large, green dustbins at the back of the flats, and broke the box as he forced it through the gap in the top.

THE TWELVE DAYS OF CHRISTMAS

Chapter 4
3rd January – ten heartfelt sorrys

Tom glanced at his watch for the fourth time. Den had been particular about meeting up at ten o'clock, and it was already twenty past. Tom could only guess that Den had patched things up with his ex-wife. If that was the case, he wouldn't be surprised if Den didn't turn up at all. It would at least make up for Tom's disappointment of being forgotten about. If, in some small way he was responsible for making the course of true love run a little bit smoother, then it was cause for a minor celebration.

As Tom sat staring at his half drunk mug of lukewarm tea, he heard the piercing sound of a car horn coming from outside. It was so loud it could easily be heard above the noise of the passing traffic. Curiosity got the better of him. He got up and walked outside the café to see Den sitting in a van across the road with another, much larger man beside him. They had stopped on a double yellow line. Before Tom could cross the road, Den had climbed out of the van and was heading towards him, with his fists clenched. He definitely didn't look a man who was loved up, unless it was some sort of angry love which Tom wasn't familiar with.

"Here he is cupid, well done, well done," Den said. He was shouting so loud it was as if he was spitting his words at Tom. "Nice one mate. Made me look like a total idiot, you…you," Den said while aggressively pointing his finger at Tom. Now Tom was a nice person, who came from a nice area and could sometimes, even by his own reckoning, be described as naive. Someone who didn't necessarily think things through before saying them. He wasn't thinking when he said, "you know what they say Den, one finger pointing at me, who are the other three pointing at?"

"You what?" Den said, distracted enough to stop what he was doing to look at his own hand.

"Just an expression. Didn't go well last night then?" Tom asked wanting to stand his ground but soon realising that he was backing up the hill towards the heath, as Den came striding towards him.

"Go round and see her, you said, wear some nice clothes, you said, give her some chocolates, you said." By this time he'd gone red in the face and because it was cold, Tom could have sworn he started to see steam coming out of Den's ears. The snow from the last few days had settled and was still piled up on the pavements and visible on the roofs of houses and some cars.

"Good job I didn't go out and buy a ring as well, isn't it."

"Excuse my ignorance Den but what actually happened last night?"

"Thanks to you I looked like a right Charlie."

"Ok, so what did you do?"

"Jeffrey was there, that's what happened. With his great big biceps and fancy spiky hair."

"Who's Jeffrey?" Tom said but his first thought was a perverse one, that he couldn't get out of his head; his dad kissing Den's ex-wife.

"I don't know do I?" Den replied rubbing his shaved head. By this time Tom had stopped his shuffle backwards and was now positioned three hundred yards away from the café, outside an electrical shop.

"What, are you telling me you went round there and you saw your ex-wife and this guy kissing?"

"Not in front of me no," Den said looking totally disgusted.

"So how do you know that he is necessarily doing anything with Yvonne?"

"I'm not an idiot am I?"

"Well did you ask?"

"Didn't know what to say did I?"

"Did you get a chance to say any of it?" There was a pause as Den's heart, which had been pumping in his chest, finally looked like it had started to calm itself. He slowly shook his head and then lowered his arm.

"Look, even if you don't get back together and there is a very real chance you won't, you need to say those things Den. I'm sorry mate but love doesn't have any guarantees. It's not like an electrical good," Tom said pointing at the window of the electrical shop, "that you can take back when it's not working and say sorry can I have a new one please. Only I broke the old ones heart but I'm hoping that if I say the magic word everything will be as good as new again." As he spoke, snow started to fall. Gently at first, but then progressively getting heavier.

"I just assumed that they were together."

"Den don't assume anything because it will make an ass out of you and me." Tom's words were unexpected and they made Den laugh but his actions were strained and within a short moment he looked like he might breakdown and cry.

"Come on Den, until you know for sure, you can't write anything off and anyway it's not necessarily about winning her back, it's about telling her that you care. Telling her that after all these years of her looking after your sons, you actually think about her and hold her in high regard and that you're sorry for treating her the way you did. Look, do you mind if we talk about this in the van?" The snow had already started to settle on their heads and the tops of their jackets.

"Yeah, it's just over…" They both turned round and saw that the van had disappeared. It was only when they went back down to the bottom of the village that they found it parked round the corner. Jack had pulled up in a lay-by opposite the station. Den lifted the hood of his sweatshirt over his head and they both made a run for it across the road. When they arrived, they found Jack tapping the steering wheel with his hands to the beat of the record on the radio.

"Do me a favour," Den said opening the driver's door of the van.

"What's that?" said Jack.

"Get out of there and wipe that smirk off your face."

"Temper, temper," replied Jack, slowly pulling himself out of the driver's seat, to be brushed aside by Den as he replaced him. Jack then went round the back of the van, opened the back door and climbed in. During which time Tom had climbed into the front passenger seat. No-one said anything for a few minutes until Jack broke the silence.

"Handbags at ten paces ehh lads?"

"Tom this is my cousin Jack. Jack this is Tom."

"Don't mind him, he's got a bit of a temper. It probably means he really likes you," explained Jack.

"I'd hate to see what he does if he doesn't like someone," replied Tom.

"Right, anyway now we've done with the pleasantries, where's Rick's place? Your mate's house?" Den said trying to deflect the attention away from himself.

"I told you before he's not my mate," Tom corrected him. "Across the river and into Fulham, should take about forty-five minutes to an hour depending on the traffic. What do we do when we get there?"

"You leave that to the experts," said Jack. Den started the van up, glanced in his wing mirror and then pulled out.

"So Tom, do you like magic tricks?"

*

"…and that's magic."

"That is really good. How did you do that? Don't you think that's great Den?"

"Not when you've seen it fifty-eight times, no."

"Ignore him," said Jack. "He's got no appreciation of the high level of skill involved." But Den didn't reply: he was too busy looking at an attractive blond woman as she strutted past the van on the other side of the road. Jack soon noticed what had caught his cousin's eye.

"Hello, hello what do we have here. Don't stare but have you seen the piece of skirt over there. Look at the pins on that," exclaimed Jack.

"Hold on, I recognise her," said Tom.

"In your dreams probably," said Jack laughing.

"Where's the camera?" said Den.

"I thought you were supposed to be in love with your ex-missus," Jack joked.

"I am. I've just got an idea. Let's just see where she goes." Den opened the shutter of Jack's digital camera and took several snaps of the woman as she walked down the road and turned to approach the door of Rick's Fulham house.

"I know, I know, that's Katrina, Chloe's best friend," Tom said, finally putting a name to the face.

"Who's Chloe?" asked Jack looking confused.

"My girlfriend, I mean ex-girlfriend," explained Tom.

"And Katrina, she's…"

"Chloe's best friend."

"So who's this Rick bloke?"

"I didn't tell you did I," commented Den. "Rick is, sorry, was Tom's best friend until he decided to have…," Den then tried to whisper in Jack's ear to avoid Tom hearing, "…some extra curricular activity with Tom's girlfriend."

"Guys, I'm sitting next to you. I heard every word of that."

"Sorry, I meant ex-girlfriend," Den said missing the point. They quickly turned their attention back to Rick's house and watched on as the front door swung open and the woman entered the house.

*

One and a half hours, eight magic tricks and two cups of tea later, Katrina eventually emerged at the door. She was entwined around Rick, who was only wearing a small white towel wrapped round his waist. They embraced in a passionate doorstep kiss. Katrina gently rubbed the hairs on his chest before walking off and waving good-bye. Den's camera finger was working overtime.

"The dirty, cheating, swine," said Tom, leaning forward in his seat. They were sitting a few hundred yards down the road, parked behind a silver Mercedes. "Can you believe that?" Although if Tom had set aside any time to think, none of it should have come as a surprise given the way Rick had acted in the past.

"Looks like old Ricky has been, what's the expression Jack?"

"Dumping on his own doorstep Den."

"That's right Jack, he's been a naughty, naughty boy."

"What do we do now?" asked Tom, who felt like he wanted shove Rick's head through another table.

"Patience Tom Kruise with a K, patience. We wait, until the coast is clear."

*

The blue overalls that Jack had given Tom to put on were at least two sizes too big and made him look ridiculous, even though he'd rolled up the legs and the sleeves. They were all trying to get changed in cramped conditions in the back of the van. Den emerged first, then Jack, carrying a box of tools and lastly Tom with a troubled expression on his face. It was beginning to dawn on him that he was about to embark on a criminal act, something that he'd never properly done before. He felt that his life was already hanging by a thin thread. One false move and the lifeline he was clinging onto could be severed in an instant, plunging him into the dark oblivion of hopelessness below.

Jack tried to shut the door, but when it wouldn't close properly he reverted to his tried and tested method of giving it a good old slam. Tom almost jumped out of his skin.

"Tom, Tom, Tom, you need to learn to chill out bro. Don't worry, we're professionals, you're in safe hands," Jack said just before he lost his footing on the edge of the curb and nearly fell over.

"Come on you two muppets we haven't got all day," Den called out from across the road. He was already close to Rick's front door. He rang the doorbell just to make sure no one else was in, having seen Rick leave with his suit on, barely ten minutes after he'd said goodbye to Katrina. Jack acted as the look out, while Den pulled out a cordless electric drill and started breaking the lock. Within minutes he'd prised open the front door and was working quickly to tackle the alarm. The noise bombarded their eardrums but barely lasted ten seconds before Den managed to immobilise it. Jack glanced at his watch.

"You must be familiar with the gaff, where should we look?" asked Den.

"What exactly are we looking for?" replied Tom.

"Evidence, either bank statements or perhaps paper work that might give us a clue. Just keep your eyes peeled," Den instructed as he walked from the hallway into the lounge. He'd already started opening the drawers of a dark wooden chest and was rummaging through them. Tom, who'd followed him in, stood over Den's shoulder and watched what he was doing. It took a moment before Den sensed his presence.

"Why don't you try the bedroom?"

If Tom had had the sense to think, he probably would have refused to venture into this area of Rick's house that could only hold painful reminders. But he was in panic mode and for every second they were in Rick's house, he felt like it was a moment too long. He now realised why he'd never turned to a life of crime, it was simply too stressful. Despite Den's clear instructions, Tom still felt like a fish out of water, unable to decide what to do next. Eventually he made his way out of the lounge, into the hallway and up the stairs. On his way, he passed the bathroom and froze when, out of the corner of his eye, he caught sight of the silhouette of a person through the frosted glass panel in the door. His heart was racing so much he began to hyperventilate. His first thought, which was a totally irrational one given what had happened, was that Chloe was in the flat. He put his hand on his chest and literally felt like he was going to collapse. He stood there frozen on the landing for several minutes, until he heard a man's voice singing to himself.

"Rock the Casbah, rock the Casbah, la la la la la don't like it, dum, dum, dum, dum dum, rock the Casbah, rock the Casbah, la la la la la don't like it."

It couldn't be Rick because they saw him leave the flat in a hurry, heading for the tube. The shadow of the person appeared right behind the frosted glass panel of the bathroom door. Tom's heart was in his mouth as the door swung open to reveal Jack standing behind it.

"Alright there Tom. You can't hang about mate come on chop chop."

"I was just off to the bedroom," Tom managed to say, after finally letting go and allowing himself to breathe properly again.

"Tough for you is it? Don't worry mate I'll come with you. I know what it's like to be dumped on by the ladies. Had plenty of experience of heartache myself. Over here is it?"

Tom nodded and Jack led the way. As they entered Rick's bedroom, or Chloe and Rick's bedroom, Tom started to get a sick feeling in the pit of his stomach. Thoughts began racing through his mind of the betrayal by his ex-best friend. Then he had a flashback of their holiday in Ibiza. The photograph of Rick and Chloe getting a little bit too close for comfort and the trust that Tom had displayed. The duplicity by Duncan, who must have known all along what had been going on but never told him, never confided in him, even though Tom had asked him outright on the train that day. Thoughts of smashing the place up were foremost in his mind. Perhaps getting a razor blade and indiscriminately shredding some of Rick's clothes.

But Tom was soon distracted from his negative thoughts by Jack.

"Look what we have here," said Jack who'd picked up a black box file, which was tucked down on the floor next to a chest of drawers. He'd opened it up and found a pile of papers.

"Aahhh," Jack said pulling out a handful of bank statements. Tom eagerly grabbed hold of them and started to flick through. He soon worked out they were in chronological order, going back several years. When Tom went to the oldest statement and started his investigation he soon found his money, posted in two instalments of seven and eight thousand pounds. He sat down on the bed and with his head and shoulders hunched over the statements, meticulously read each one. In the meantime Jack kept looking round the room. Every now and then he'd pick something up and inspect it, distracting himself without actually doing anything useful. Tom noticed that in one month Chloe had taken five trips to the hairdressers, had eight expensive meals and he lost count of the amount spent in various department stores.

"She's been, she's been…," Tom tried to talk, despite hitting an emotional low point.

"…living the life of Riley," finished off Jack, looking at the statements over his shoulder.

"Yeah basically. She's taken me for a ride."

"Try not to feel too upset," said Jack, "you're not the first bloke to be used by a woman and you certainly won't be the last. I remember Gloria as if it was yesterday. I spent a fortune on her last Christmas and when I say a fortune I mean a lot of dough. Hundreds of pounds on clothes and little nick-nacks. In fact, it was the nick-nacks that cost the most."

"What happened to her?" Tom asked, searching for an anecdote that would give him a crumb of comfort, feeling like a capsized man left floating in the middle of a cold and hostile ocean, clinging onto a sinking life raft, praying for the rescue ship to arrive.

"Ran off with her badminton partner, Ralph. I knew they were up to something more than just hitting shuttlecocks if you know what

I mean. Worst thing of all, what really really got to me was that he pretended to be interested in my magic tricks. Now that is low."

After carefully inspecting every single item on the bank statements, Tom eventually let his hand fall slowly onto the bed.

"Come on Tom, let's go and tell Den about what we've found. The sooner we get out of this place, the better it will be for you."

*

When they got back to the lounge they found Den sitting on the sofa, with a laptop open on the coffee table, typing away.

"This is no time to surf the net cuz, look what we found," Jack said showing Den the bank statements.

"Nice one, anything interesting?"

"Looks like she's been taking the Michael, good and proper," explained Jack.

"Tom could you do us a favour?" Den asked employing a manner that was unusually polite. "Would you mind going upstairs and double checking all the other rooms, just in case there's something we've missed?"

"Ok," Tom said looking at Den suspiciously, before obediently trotting into the hallway and back up the stairs.

"Check he's gone will you?" asked Den. Jack went to the doorway and quickly glanced up and down the hallway.

"Yep, why?"

"Come and have a butchers at this." Jack made his way over to the sofa. By the time he got there Den had turned the laptop round on the coffee table so that Jack could see the screen.

"I didn't have you down as a good Samaritan."

"Just trying to give the truth a gentle nudge."

"Breaking a nut with a sledge hammer more like. Is this her PC then?"

"What the pink one? Yes I'm making the rather bold assumption that it's Chloe's and not Ricky's computer."

"Come on, let's get hold of Tom and get out of here. I don't think we'll be able to recoup much of his money."

"She's certainly taken him for a ride, hasn't she?"

"She has cuz. But what goes around comes around," Den said as he switched off the laptop, closed the lid and carefully wiped it down with a cloth he had in his jacket pocket. "What goes around comes around."

*

Tom made his way up to the top floor of Rick's house. For some reason he felt drawn to the small spare box room at the end of the hallway, like a moth to a light bulb. He switched the hall light on and slowly made his way towards the door. Despite everything that he'd already found out he was still genuinely quite shocked at what he discovered when he opened it. Hundreds and hundreds of boxes, neatly stacked almost three-quarters of the way up to the ceiling. He randomly picked one half way down, gently prizing it free of all the others, trying to avoid being buried alive in a potential avalanche of boxes. 'Jimmy Choo' was written down the side in gold lettering. He opened it up and inside was an expensive, dainty looking pair of black, pointed women's shoes with straps. Tom then continued to indiscriminately pull out boxes and check the contents. It turned out that Chloe had accumulated the largest collection of shoes he'd ever seen, large enough to make Imelda Marcos blush.

*

"Just remember to tell her that you're sorry, you know, if that's how you really feel. It's got to come from the heart, Den. You've got to get in touch with how you really feel."

"Well, I miss her and I miss the boys and this guilt, well it's eating me up inside."

"Then that's what you've got to tell her."

"What if Jeffery's there?" Den said.

"Tell him to take a hike," chipped in Jack, who was sitting next to Den in the driver's seat.

"I heard that. Thanks for the input Jack but no don't tell him to take a hike, just ask her politely if you could have a word in private."

"What if she doesn't want to?"

"Come on Den, you must have talked your way in and out of trickier situations than this. Use that East London charm. It was probably what attracted her to you in the first place."

"Yeah, probably," Den said allowing himself a brief smile.

"Be honest and don't expect anything, ok."

"Ok," acknowledged Den.

"Good luck and I'll catch up with you tomorrow," rounded off Tom.

"See you later," replied Den before switching his mobile phone off and then shoving it in his pocket. He put on his black woolly hat and zipped up his green bomber jacket. This time he'd left the smart trousers and itchy shirt where they belonged, in the bottom drawer of his chest. It was going to be him as he is, take him or leave him.

"Break a leg," said Jack "and remember the offer's still there."

"What, the one where if I fail to get back with Yvonne I can still elope with you."

"Always good to have a plan B," replied Jack.

"Thanks for the lift," said Den.

"No problemo, give us a yell if you need picking up later."

"Will do."

The van door seemed heavier than usual as Den had to summon his energy to slowly push it open and make the long, solitary walk to the lift. The snow made the concrete surface slippery under his feet and he had to watch his footing.

As he approached the front door, his heart started racing again and he was having trouble breathing. He prayed that Jeffery wasn't there. Once he was in front of the door, despite the biting cold, he couldn't bring himself to knock. It swung open of its own accord, the light pouring out, illuminating the darkness around him and making Den feel like he was standing at the entrance of an Aladdin's cave. There, dressed in his Spiderman outfit stood his youngest son, Freddie. He was holding a broken action man in his left hand.

"Dad, I knew it was you." Freddie turned round and shouted, "mum, mum you've got someone here to see you."

"How did you know that it was me, you little rascal?" Den said ruffling Freddie's hair.

"Stop it dad."

"Freddie how many times have I told you not to answer the door to strangers."

"Hi Yvonne."

"Twice in two days Den, you can't seem to stay away."

"Can I come in and have a word, assuming you're on your own."

"Yes I'm on my own."

"What about Jeffery, not around then?" Den couldn't help himself.

"If I didn't know you better Dennis Johnston, I'd guess that you were a teeny weeny bit jealous."

"No, I just don't think he looked, well, that he's good enough for you."

"Come in Den it's freezing outside," Yvonne said, grabbing hold of Den's arm and pulling him inside. Freddie ran ahead of them and then swerved into the lounge.

"Cup of tea?"

"Yeah please," even though he could have done with something stronger.

"Still on the wagon then?"

"Yeah pretty much."

Yvonne raised her eyebrows and gave him one of her disapproving expressions.

"Ok, look I've decided that from now on I'm going to be honest with you, ok. I reckon that's the only way you're ever going to trust me again."

"And?" she said putting a tea bag in each of the two cups in front of her.

"I had a drink on the day before New Year's Eve, dad's birthday, and I didn't stop until I was thrown in prison on New Year's morning".

"When are you ever going to learn, you're just like…," but she stopped short of saying what he expected her to. "What for?"

"This idiot spilt my drink and I had a rush of blood to my head."

"Den, I'm so sorry," she said with a look of compassion in her eyes. It wasn't something he'd seen from her in years and it was totally unexpected. He'd braced himself for a good dressing down.

"Why are you sorry?"

"Because I know how much it still hurts you. What happened with your dad."

"Yeah, look I'm not here to talk about that. I've got something I need to say to you."

"Let's sit down," she said gesturing towards the kitchen table.

"The boys alright?"

"Yes, I let them stay up on a Friday and watch telly, as a treat if they've been good. They usually are, bless them. They showed me the paintings you did with them."

"Did they? I forgot about that."

"I didn't know you could paint."

"Can't really."

"Well I appreciate it, you know, you doing that with them."

"It's not much. To be honest the person who deserves the praise is you. You're a good mother, do you know that?"

"I do my best," she said trying not to get emotional.

"I really mean that."

"What's happened Den, you're not in trouble are you?"

"No, well no nothing like that, I just wanted to say, to say that," he took a deep breath and paused before letting it all out.

"I'm sorry. Sorry for being drunk for the last nine years. Sorry for never telling you how special you are to me. Sorry for not being there when you needed me the most. Sorry for the times I let you down. Sorry for the times I let the boys down. Sorry for the time I hit you. Sorry for the money that I never gave you but spent on booze and gambling. Sorry for not being there when you gave birth to Freddie. Sorry for telling your mother I hated her when she was just protecting you and sorry for never protecting you myself."

After never being able to say it, it was like Den had opened up the flood gates and when he did, so did Yvonne. The tears at first started to make her eyes glisten but then began to stream down her cheeks in lines; splashing on the kitchen table. She started sobbing uncontrollably, as if she'd been holding onto the hurt all these years, waiting to release the pain and heartache of nearly a decade. For once Den instinctively knew what to do. He got up off the kitchen chair, knelt down to the side of her and put his arm around her. While they embraced she gently kissed him on the cheek.

"Are you sure Jeffery won't get jealous?"

"He's my hairdresser you idiot, and he's gay just in case you were wondering," Yvonne said poking him quite hard in the ribs.

Crouched outside the kitchen door, Freddie and Kevin were listening to every word. Despite the tears in their eyes, there was a smile on both of their faces. It was the best present they could ever wish for.

"I knew it," whispered Kevin, "I knew it."

Chapter 5
January 4th – eleven other victims

Tom sat in the café hunched over his mug of tea, not keen to face up to reality in any way, shape or form. He contemplated ordering another drink but once again caught himself staring at the bottom of his empty cup. He slowly looked up when he felt the presence of someone standing over him.

"What are you so happy about? No, let me guess. You ended up knocking seven bells out of Jeffery," Tom said forcing a smile at his own comment.

"Me, a man of violence?" Den said trying to look as if butter wouldn't melt in his mouth.

"No, you're right. I must be getting you confused with what's-his-name, that Nelson Mandela."

"I'll have you know Mr Mandela liked a bit of trouble in his younger days. And anyway it just so happens that my old pal Jeffrey is a life long member of the Barry Manilow fan club, if you get my drift."

"Right, so come on, spill the beans."

"Well, I gave it to her straight. I told her that I was a changed man. As you would expect there were a lot of tears."

"…on his part," interrupted Jack, chuckling to himself. He appeared moments after Den. "Cried like a baby apparently. Did a great impression of Niagara Falls from what I heard."

"Give it a rest, Jack Blaine." They both sat down together, Den taking the seat opposite Tom.

"Did you say you were sorry?"

"Yeah, yeah, I told her that I'd been contemplating the error of my ways."

"And?"

"She said, well she said that it was early days but that she still had feelings for me."

"Have they ordered the guide dog for her yet?" commented Jack with a mischievous expression on his face.

"Shut your cakehole," Den replied, momentarily switching his attention towards his cousin.

"She wants to take it easy but the long and the short of it is, she can't resist the old Dennis the Menace charm."

"Good for you," Tom said offering his hand to be shaken.

"Thanks," said Den, grabbing hold and shaking Tom's hand vigorously.

"That's alright I didn't do much," Tom said modestly.

"No you're right, it was all me," Den said grinning back.

*

"Right I'm going to go through this one last time, for the hard of hearing," Den turned round and looked at Jack and Tom for some sort of confirmation that they knew what he was asking them to do. They were both sitting on upturned crates in the back of the van, dressed in blue overalls.

"Me and Jack will see if he's in. You stay in the van. Out of sight," Den said looking at Tom. "If he's not there then I'll give you the signal.

Actually, come to think of it, you got those wigs?"

"Yes, hold on," Jack said moving off his crate and fumbling around the back of the van. "Here they are."

"Good you put that one on and, just to be safe, the tash as well."

"Are you taking the pee?" replied Tom, thinking that this was their way of having a laugh at his expense.

"No Tom, I'm extremely serious. It's for your own protection. Anything goes wrong and someone clocks you, then the chances are they won't recognise you with that on."

"What, the blond guy with the stupid moustache."

"Better than the stupid guy without a wig and tash in prison. I thought that you might have had enough of that place."

"Anyway you're not the only one," Den said nodding in Jack's direction. When Tom turned round he was greeted with the sight of Jack wearing a brown curly haired wig, a baseball cap and a big bushy moustache.

"We look like Starsky and Hutch."

"More like Cannon and Ball if you ask me," Den said. "Right, is there anything else?"

"The signal," Tom said sounding a bit anxious.

"Yes ok, when I think it's safe, I'll put my toolbox down on the ground."

"Ok," acknowledged Tom.

"And you Jack?"

"What?"

"What have you got to remember?"

"To let you do all the talking."

"And, what in particular?"

"Not to mention David Blaine."

"Fantastic, I love it when a plan comes together."

"Right gents, I expect that this job is going to be a little bit more tricky than yesterday's, most likely. Looking at the alarm cover on the wall over there I'd say it's a lot more sophisticated, may even be one of those American subsonic devices. It doesn't give us that much time."

"Did you just make that up?" asked Jack.

"No."

"Well it sounds like you made it up."

"What are we looking for?" Tom said trying to steer them away from their argument.

"Same as before. Evidence that you've been led up the garden path. I've got a sneaky suspicion that your ex-business partner has wandered from the path of righteousness many times in the past. In my experience, people like him who get away with it for a while, tend to get sloppy. Often make a few schoolboy errors: leave documents lying around, something like that."

"Ok," replied Tom thoughtfully.

"Right let's go." Den climbed out the van and slammed the door shut. Jack joined him by climbing out the back of the van.

The place that Raymond lived in was a large, detached house in a quiet road in Beckenham, Kent. The snow appeared to be thicker in this area than in Central London and was at least a foot deep, covering every inch of the roof and extensive grounds. It gave the place a fairy tale appearance. Tom recalled the house from the time he was there a few years ago, when he was invited to play tennis with Raymond and sign the business contract, which made them partners.

He remembered that day vividly because Raymond annihilated him on the tennis court without even breaking into a sweat. Tom hit so many balls out of the court, that at one point, it looked like they might run out. After the game Tom signed and handed over a cheque for £10,000. If Den was right, and Tom was beginning to believe that he was, then Raymond had played him for a fool. It was a hard lesson to learn on top of the ones that Chloe and Rick had already dished out. It was dawning on him that he simply didn't know these people. Most of the relationships in his life had been built on sand.

Tom refocused his attention on his new found friends Den and Jack, who'd now reached the front door of the Georgian white washed house and were ringing the doorbell. Den turned round and looked over in the direction of the van. He slowly and purposefully lowered his tool bag and put it on the ground. Tom waited a moment while Jack tried the door bell once more and then went round the side of the house to see if anyone was there. He then got out of the back of the van, but in the time it took for him to do this Den had picked his toolbox up again. Tom momentarily panicked, hesitated, then opened the van door and got back in. Once inside the back of the van, he got himself in a position where he could see Den and Jack. He noticed that he'd put the toolbox down again. Then he could see that they were pointing over in his direction and looked like they were holding onto their stomachs. It was then that Tom realised they were laughing at him.

"That's not funny," Tom said to himself, whilst climbing out of the van. He then made his way over to where they were standing, turning back to lock the van using the electronic key. On the way Tom's mind was working overtime, thinking of as many different ways as he could, to take his revenge.

"Got ya," said Den smiling.

"Very amusing," acknowledged Tom.

"Come on Tom, what have you been waiting for, we've been ready for ages," said Den.

"I'll get you for this, maybe not now, maybe not here but I'll get you, when you least expect it."

"I'm quaking in my boots," said Den, quickly grabbing hold of Jack and pretending to hide behind him.

"Anyway, less of the joking around, we've got some serious business to do. Are you ready Den?" asked Jack.

"As ready as I'll ever be." Jack pulled out a screwdriver, a pair of wire cutters, and then a leather pouch which he proceeded to unfold to reveal an array of metal implements of varying shapes and sizes. He quickly bent down and went to work on the front door. Den rubbed his chin and contemplated for a moment on how to bypass the alarm. Tom stood around feeling like a spare part.

Within moments Jack had got the door open. Like before, when they'd broken into Rick's house, the alarm made a loud, piercing sound that instantly made them want to put their hands over their ears. Den was quickly inside and within a minute, and several clicks of his wire cutters, all was quiet again and the sleepy corner of suburbia which they were in, was filled back up to the rim with tranquillity.

Once inside, all three men marvelled at the opulence of Raymond's house. Georgian elegance with wooden and marble flooring but combined with modern technology, from plasma TV screens to touch sensor lighting. The double height ceilings and the intricacies of the plastered cornice made it feel like every room was a unique, vast space to be admired and enjoyed.

"What did you say this bloke did again?"

"Well he told me he was an entrepreneur. The expression he used was some fingers in a few pies."

"Must have been some pretty big pies if you ask me. His hallway is bigger than my flat," said Jack while looking closely at a marble bust of a Roman looking man.

"Where's the safe?" asked Den.

"Right, that's in the study, which is this way," Tom said taking charge, finally feeling he was useful for something. He led them down the hallway which then opened up into a large atrium, with the most amazing set of staircases to the left and right, curling round and meeting in the middle to form an internal balcony. On the floor was an intricate marble mosaic design. He then took them under the staircase and through to a door, which was closed but not locked. When they walked in, directly in front of them, was a huge bookcase that covered almost the entire back wall, made of walnut coloured wood. The books were leather bound and in neat sets. They looked too pristine to be for anything other than decoration.

"Come over here," beckoned Tom, as he walked up to the bookcase. "Give me a minute, it's one of these." He then started pulling out books on the two middle shelves, until one showed some degree of resistance. "Are you watching this?" Tom said to his friends who were still taking in the grandness of the setting. Tom pulled the group of books forward like pulling a lever and the painting on the far wall, of a fox hunt, slowly moved to the right to reveal a shiny, chrome safe.

"Raymond couldn't resist showing me this. He'd had it installed the week before we set up the galleries."

"Well looks like Raymond's got a bit careless already, doesn't it," commented Den.

Jack laid down his rucksack on the wooden floor and pulled out his black leather pouch again. He carefully unravelled it to reveal various tools, drill bits and a stethoscope.

"How long do you reckon?"

"How long is a piece of string?," replied Jack.

"As long as you cut it," said Den.

"Precisely."

"So…"

"I really don't know," Jack replied getting a bit frustrated with his cousin's persistent questions.

"Come on Tom, why don't we check the rest of the gaff out. I'm keen to know where the billiard room is," Den said jovially slapping Tom on the back.

"I thought you weren't into breaking open safes."

"That's right, more into blowing them open," Den said laughing.

"What? You mean he's going to used explosives? Have you gone completely mad?"

"You didn't think we were going to spring it open with our skill and expertise at cracking ten digit codes, did you?"

"Well, yes actually, I thought you might, you know, break the code or something."

"I'm sorry but this isn't a Bond movie Tom, this is real life."

*

Jack pulled out his drilling equipment from the nylon zip bag and quietly pieced it together. He mounted it on a collapsible, lightweight, metal stand, which he'd assembled in a matter of minutes by pulling the rope that was threaded through the middle of it. He unscrewed the adjusters so that it was the correct height, made one more final check with the measurements he'd written down and then flicked the switch to begin drilling. The low whirring noise turned into a high pitched scream, as the drill touched the surface of the shiny metal safe. Jack used his not insubstantial frame to try and ease the metal drill piece further into the door, but after a few minutes it had barely made a scratch.

He stopped drilling and pulled out the drill bit using a cloth, as it was, by this stage, too hot to handle. He then inserted a much sharper and more durable bit into the drill. This time he was more successful, making a hole big enough to plant the small amount of explosives necessary to blow the safe door open. At least that's what he hoped would happen. Funnily enough, the explosives he'd managed to get hold of didn't come with any written instructions. The one thing he didn't want to do, was to use too much and destroy the safe's contents.

Out of a smaller bag, Jack removed a tiny metal box containing the explosives. It looked like a lump of soft, grey plasticine, which he moulded into the hole he'd just drilled. A bead of sweat, which had spent the last few minutes forming on his head, fell onto his hand as he methodically went about his business. Jack deftly fixed the tiny detonator, which was shaped like a small metal bolt, into the heart of the explosive. He quickly unravelled the red wire which was just long enough to allow him to hide behind Raymond's writing desk, over by the window. After attaching the wires to a large battery, he then flicked open a black plastic case to reveal a red button.

"You were only supposed to blow the bloody doors off," he said to himself after the concussive force and sound of the explosion made Jack partially deaf for a few minutes. A large puff of grey smoke shot out from the safe, filling the air in the study and at the same time filling Jack with dread, as he immediately thought he'd used too much. He placed his hand over his mouth and nose and used his other hand to wave a path between himself and the safe. As Jack pulled on the metal lever the door sprung open. Inside were dozens and dozens of thick bundles of twenty and fifty pound notes, loosely thrown on top of a pile of brown folders. There was also a large red velvet box. Jack quickly grabbed hold of all the bundles of money and piled them into the nearest rucksack. Within seconds of hiding all the money, Den and Tom appeared through the doorway.

"Jack, couldn't you have done that more quietly?"

"There are, I'm afraid, no quiet ways of blowing open a safe, cuz," explained Jack.

"What have you found?" asked Den.

"I found these," Jack said handing him the sizeable, brown, A4 folders. Each one had a name on the front. 'Abra-kebabra' was written on the one at the top, 'Tantastic' on the next, 'Davy Jones's Locker' and so on.

"Right, what was the name of your company again?"

"Kruise Galleries. Not that original I know but, when I was thinking of a name, a lot of the ones I really liked had already been taken and I kind of wanted it to represent..."

"Well have a butchers at that." Den said interrupting Tom by handing him a folder with his company's name typed on it in big, black bold lettering. Den quickly looked through the rest of the folders in the pile. Tom unhooked the elastic that was holding the contents of the file together. Inside was a detailed listing of every single transaction that his galleries had made since the company was first founded. At the bottom was an accumulated profits total of just under £50,000. Den, who was looking over Tom's shoulder, couldn't hold back a smile.

"I knew it, didn't I tell you. Use your accountant to hide the profits and then tell the punter you're legging over that they've got debts of the same amount. Very neat and tidy. Tom stood in Raymond's house wearing a blond wig and a matching moustache, with oversized blue overalls and he didn't just look a fool, he felt like one as well. But before another word could be said all three jumped when they heard a bang on the front door.

"Who the hell?" Jack said anxiously.

"Don't panic it's probably just a neighbour wondering what the noise was," suggested Den. As they got closer to the front door, they heard voices.

"Open up," came the man's voice, "it's the police." Jack ran back to the study, closely followed by Den and Tom. He bent down, frantically trying to take his drill apart and dismantle his equipment.

"Leave it," Den said in a harsh whisper. "Just make sure there are no prints on it."

"I can't," replied Jack, the worry visible in his eyes and in his erratic movements. After giving up unscrewing his equipment he turned his attention on trying to force the velvet box into the top of his rucksack but it was a few inches too wide to fit. He finally gave up when Den grabbed hold of the back of his jacket and pulled him to his feet.

"I said, leave it. We haven't got time," reiterated Den.

They collected what they could and Den led them out through the lounge and into the dining room, to a pair of large glass French doors which went out onto the patio and garden. He undid the bolts at the top and bottom and then turned the key which had been left in the lock. As he opened the door and stepped out onto the enormous patio, two policemen appeared about five hundred yards away, coming round the side of the house.

"Run for it," shouted Den, who led the way by sprinting out into the garden which, until Den disturbed it, was covered by a carpet of white snow. Tom and Jack followed closely behind him. Tom was helping Jack carry one of his rucksacks, the contents of which were bouncing up and down as they jogged along. The first policeman, the older of the two, began speaking into his walkie talkie, which was attached to his jacket.

- "We are in pursuit of three suspects at 83 Havenport Gardens," officer Nigel shouted into his radio as he and his colleague, Charlie, darted across the lawn and past a large stone statue of a man that looked remarkably like Raymond.

"8…3…Havenport, that's H for Hotel, A for Alpha, V for Victor, E for Echo, N for November…," panted Nigel as he struggled to keep up. At the far end of the garden was a large wooden screen which was used to separate the lawn from the woodland behind it. Den, who was desperately thinking about how they were going to escape, had a moment of inspiration.

"Follow me," he said, glancing back at Tom and Jack who were several paces behind him. All three disappeared behind the screen and then ran the whole length to get to the other end. Den stopped and then waited for the policeman to catch up. Charlie was the first to arrive, having taken the lead over his older colleague who was finding it difficult to keep up.

"What are you doing?" asked Tom panting heavily.

"We've got to get back to the van," explained Den. As soon as the younger of the two policemen reached the other end of the screen, Den started running, doubling back towards the house. Nigel looked the most surprised as he watched the three criminals heading back in his direction. At this point Charlie had almost caught up on Jack, who was moving awkwardly and running out of steam. Nigel was going to try and intercept them but had second thoughts when he saw Jack coming towards him, with a less than welcoming expression on his face. He watched on as they ran by, about twenty yards away from him. The more youthful Charlie wasn't so cautious and just before they reached the house, he made his move.

"Stop. Police." was all that he could muster, in between heavy pants. Charlie made his announcement before hurling himself at Jack and landing on his back. Jack looked like he didn't know what to do with the policeman who was acting like a cowboy attempting to ride a bucking bronco. The extra weight soon bought Jack to a standstill.

"Get rid of that thing on your back," shouted Den, who could see that this was messing up his escape plan.

"I'm trying," said Jack, his voice slightly muffled by the policeman who had his arm wrapped around his throat. Jack dropped his shoulder and lunged his body to the left and then to the right and back again. Charlie was being tossed in the air like a limp rag doll. His feet were off the ground as Jack began spinning round and at the same time, loosening the policeman's grip. Seconds later Charlie went flying through the air, his fall being broken by a spiky looking exotic plant, half covered in the snow.

"Come on, stop mucking around," said Den as he saw that the second policeman had managed to catch up with his colleague.

"Man down," said Nigel into his walkie talkie, desperately trying not to sound too dramatic. "Please send assistance, in pursuit of criminals in Havenport Gardens. I repeat man down."

Den knew that having dealt with the immediate problem of the two policemen, the situation would get much worse when more followed. He led Jack and Tom round the side of the house and through the gate. Den stopped to have a quick look up and down the road. When he saw all was clear, he headed straight for the van. He then quickly opened the back door, threw in his shoulder bag, ran round the front and jumped into the driver's seat. Jack and Tom dived head first, bags and all, into the back of the van.

"Drive," shouted Jack, in between gasping for air. The tightness in his chest was making him squirm. Den started the engine and then floored the accelerator. The tyres initially struggled to grip the tarmac. The snow had compressed under the wheels. When the van did respond, it skidded and as soon as Den started driving he lost control, almost hitting a nearby parked car before regaining his composure. Tom was still preoccupied by his efforts to shut the van doors properly and almost fell out of the back as the van jolted forward. In fact when Den swerved sharply it was only the door handle, which Tom clung onto, that prevented him from dropping out onto the road. As he hung halfway out, Jack had to use all his strength as he grabbed hold of his legs and pulled him back in. As they drove round the next corner they nearly collided with a police car head on. It swerved to get out of the way and slide into the back of a parked BMW. The impact set off the parked car's alarm. Den reacted by veering to his left and in the process scraped the side of a white van that was parked on the other side of the road.

"Watch out" shouted Jack, when he saw another car coming towards them. He was kneeling down in the back of the van, peering out between the head rests. Den gestured with his hand to the driver to get out of the way as he soon realised he had no chance of stopping in time.

When the driver coming towards them failed to react, Den had no choice but to put his foot on the accelerator and try and squeeze through the gap between the oncoming car and the parked car ahead. He wanted to close his eyes but instead ended up squinting. More through luck than judgment, he made it through the gap by a fraction of a centimetre. Den then had to put his foot on the brake to try and avoid skidding, as he approached a sharp bend in the road.

"What are we going to do?" asked Jack as he sat back down in the van, with his back against the side.

"Not panic, that's what we're going do," replied Den with a determined expression on his face. He glanced in the wing mirror and could see that for the moment at least, no-one was trying to follow them.

Den's mind was working overtime. The police could have seen the number plates. His first thought was they must get rid of the van, and quick. That was the only link between them and the burglary. Perhaps the best thing would be to ditch it; set fire to it.

"They probably didn't get a proper look at us because of the disguises right?," Den said, searching for confirmation.

"It's unlikely," agreed Jack.

"All they've got to trace us with is a rough idea of our heights, and weight. And the van."

"But we've got other plates in the lock up and we could spray it with a new coat of paint."

"Yeah but that's risky. What if they catch us doing it? We could just ditch it."

"Trouble is, it's got our fingerprints all over it. I say give it a good clean, spray paint it and we don't use it for a few months."

"Good skills with the copper by the way. He went flying into that bush."

"Yeah I reckon he'll be walking funny for the next few days."

"More than a few days I reckon. Bought a tear to my eye that did."

They all started to laugh. Even Tom, who'd hardly said a word since they'd been forced to leave the house, burst into laughter. Up until this point his mind had been elsewhere: on what to do with all the information he had in his rucksack and how to get his money back. If they could get out of this then he was beginning to realise there weren't that many options open to him, other than blackmail. Tom had always thought of himself as a nice guy but what good had it done him? Perhaps it's true what they say nice guys do always finish last.

*

After ditching the overalls and disguises in a large bin round the back of a restaurant in Lee Park, Jack and Den dropped Tom off as close to Blackheath as they dare risk before making their way through the back streets to their lockup. They agreed that it was best to split up and lie low. Deny everything if they were asked any questions. Make sure that they all had an alibi. It was a reminder to Tom that he was short on people that he could really trust and the only person who came to mind was his sister. Although he didn't have a criminal record, Tom did have a motive and the police wouldn't have to dig too deep into Raymond's affairs to get evidence. Not that Raymond would be too keen to pursue this any further, given his murky past.

By the time Tom had got back to his flat, had a shower and a cup of tea, he'd decided what he was going to do. He flipped open his mobile phone and scrolled down to find Raymond's number. It rang for what seemed like an eternity and Tom almost gave up before Raymond finally answered.

"Hello," came the distinctive, bellowing voice.

"Hello Raymond," said Tom in an 'I know what you've been up to' kind of way.

"Who's that?"

"Don't you recognise me? It hasn't been that long." Tom had seen enough movies where the blackmailer plays sinister games with his victim.

"Well it sounds like Tom Kruise, but why are you talking that way." Raymond's sharp reply unsettled Tom.

"I need to talk to you, face to face."

"Can't it wait, I've just found out I've been burgled."

"I'm sorry to hear that," Tom said smiling. "Hope they didn't get much."

"Well it's too early to say," Raymond replied sounding quite cagey. There was a pause.

"No, I'm afraid it can't wait," Tom eventually said steering the conversation. "I think you'll be very interested to hear what I have to say," even though at this stage he didn't actually have a clue what he was going to talk about.

"You're being very enigmatic."

"Am I?" Tom said, not exactly sure what enigmatic meant. Then, he panicked thinking that Raymond might know more about the burglary than he was letting on.

"Well I didn't mean to be. Do they know who did it? The burglary," he said changing the subject.

"The police told me they caught them in the act, apparently, but they managed to escape. They've got descriptions. An odd looking bunch by all accounts. You know what these criminals are like, so stupid they're bound to leave some clue or other. I wouldn't want to be in their shoes if the police catch them. As well as burglary, they resisted arrest and assaulted a police officer. Not to mention blowing up my safe."

"Oh no, not your lovely chrome one."

"Couldn't get it open any other way. What they didn't realise was that it was wired to the police station."

"Really."

"Yes, look I don't mean to be rude but I am rather busy at the moment. Couldn't you just tell me whatever it is over the phone?"

"Tell you what?" Tom replied, momentarily forgetting why he'd phoned up in the first place.

"Well whatever it is that's so urgent that you need to speak to me face to face."

"No, I need to see you."

"Ok well the police have finally finished dusting for finger prints. Is six o'clock alright with you, round my place? Do you remember where it is?"

"Oh yes, see you at six."

*

Tom was standing in Raymond's messed up study staring at the open door of his safe. The black charcoal stains were spread like spilt ink over the clean crisp wall. It was more than a bit unnerving returning to the scene of his crime. On the table were copies of photofits that the police were circulating.

"Those don't look anything like us," Tom said under his breath.

"What was that?" asked Raymond, who was standing behind Tom.

"What a mess?" I said.

"Yes I agree with you there."

"Still they didn't get much, did they?" Tom probed.

"Look what is it you're being so mysterious about. As you can see I've got a lot on my plate at the moment."

"Well, how can I put this?" Tom said clearing his throat. He'd never been very good at confronting people.

"Plain and simply and well quickly, if you don't mind," replied Raymond. Rather than upsetting Tom, Raymond's arrogant attitude spurred him on. Raymond strolled over to his drinks cabinet and started pouring himself a glass of whiskey.

"I know what you've been up to, with your little scam."

"What do you mean, scam?" Raymond replied, the expression on his face showed that he was finally taking Tom seriously.

"Well, what if I told you there's nothing wrong with my business. That the £50,000 debt is a fabrication and that actually it has made that amount in profits."

"I'd say that you've been smoking those funny cigarettes again."

"Oh really, I'm sure that the police might want to know what I'm talking about. Perhaps I could hang around and wait for the Detective Inspector to turn up," Tom said settling himself behind the desk that was positioned towards the back of the study. The leather creaked as he sat on the swivel chair. At that moment Tom was very tempted to see if he could put his knees up and by leveraging himself off the desk, spin all the way round.

"You know that you're being naive, Tom. You'd do well not to poke your nose in where it doesn't belong and make idle threats. People in glass houses…"

"What about them?"

"…shouldn't throw stones."

"Well that makes sense, only a fool would do that."

"It's an expression," Raymond said getting impatient.

"Are you implying that I've got skeletons in my closet?"

"What I'm saying is, it's getting late and if you don't mind…"

"Still, like I said, nice little scam you got going," Tom repeated, growing in confidence. "Got to give you credit for that, simple but effective. Get some unsuspecting mug like myself to invest in a business. Find yourself a less than scrupulous accountant. Cook the books. Make it look like there's a loss. Pocket all the money and if they're really stupid enough to try and inject a bit of cash to save their business, more fool them. Heads you win, tails they lose. Very clever, you just didn't bargain on one thing…"

"What's that?"

"Someone uncovering evidence of your goings on. A record of every transaction. All that would be required for a conviction. Especially if you'd done it quite a few times, say eleven."

"So you broke into my house?"

"No, no, no, no, no, no, no who would be that stupid?" Tom said pointing at his head.

"Well if it was you, what the hell are you doing here? You've got all my spare cash. Have you just come to gloat, is that it?"

"What do you mean, cash?"

"The money, the £100,000 I had in my safe," Raymond exclaimed, his cheeks red with anger. Tom didn't reply, he just stared at Raymond in disbelief.

*

"Come on, pick up the phone," Tom shouted in frustration. When it went through to Den's mobile answer machine for the third time, he finally decided to leave a message. "Calm down, calm down," he said to himself. He took a deep breath and tried to gain his composure.

"Look I know about the money. I know that you and Jack are probably at the airport, off to sun yourselves on some beach in an exotic location and well, I just wanted to say I don't blame you. That's all, and well, I realise I don't know where you live or where Jack lives or where your lock-up is, so we probably won't see each other again, but I really thought you were my friend, that you both were. I hope that you and Yvonne work it all out and you get to go on that holiday to Italy now. Oh it's Tom by the way."

Tom's granddad Albert used to say, you come into this world with nothing and you leave with nothing. Tom was just hoping that for at least some of the time he was here, he was going to have a bit more than nothing. Unfortunately, from where he was standing, things weren't looking great.

Chapter 6
January 5th – twelve reasons why

Tom was in a reflective mood. He went to the fridge and was tempted to pour himself a large measure of vodka. Instead he grabbed hold of an unopened cartoon of milk, opting for a hot, sweet cup of tea. As he stood in his kitchen a shiver ran though his body. So while the kettle was boiling, he walked through to the bedroom to turn the heating up.

On the way, he passed two photographs, mounted in matching black picture frames, sitting on top of his chest of drawers. Both had Chloe in them. One of them was taken when they went to ski school, on holiday in Meribel, in the French Alps and the other showed them at a bar in the West End of London. He pulled open the top drawer of his chest and in one swift motion, swept them with his arm into the half filled space and firmly pushed it shut. Tom then walked back into the kitchen, made up his mug of tea and took it into the lounge to settle on the sofa. Funnily enough, as he reflected on recent events it wasn't Chloe, or Duncan or even Rick that occupied his thoughts, but the way that Den had acted. He was really disappointed in him. Not that Tom blamed him, after all it was a life changing sum of money even split two ways. The thing that really hurt Tom was that he finally thought he'd met someone that he could trust, even after such a short time. A person who cared enough to help him get passed his old demons: taking him to the grave of his dead sister, and then asking him how he felt about it.

"Buzz," went the intercom system. It made a sharp, loud noise which made Tom jump. He took a quick sip of his tea, placed it on his coffee table and then made his way to a small TV screen mounted on the wall in the hallway. His heart nearly missed a beat when he recognised the face of the woman standing in front of the camera. What the hell did she want?

"Tom, are you there? Tom please pick up it's really important."

"What do you want?"

"Look, well, I'm really upset," and then the waterworks started. "I just need someone to, talk to." Tom paused for a second and then buzzed Chloe in. In no time he heard her footsteps as she made her way up the corridor from the lifts. Tom was so indecisive about the whole thing, having let her in the building he wasn't sure if he wanted to open the door but as with most things relating to Chloe, he soon caved in.

"Hi Tom," Chloe said dabbing her eyes with a tissue. She went to hug him.

"Hi Chloe," replied Tom. There was an uncomfortable moment when she half flung herself at him but Tom, unsure of how to react, almost side-stepped out of her way.

"I'm sorry it was unexpected, it was just, well I was in the neighbourhood and I really needed someone to talk to."

"Shouldn't you be, I don't know, busy arranging wedding things," Tom said bitterly.

She stared at him for a moment, mascara running down her cheeks and then blurted out, "The wedding's off."

"It's what?" Tom said almost breaking out into a smile but quickly adjusting the expression on his face to something more serious.

"Rick, he, he…" and then the floodgates opened again. Tom ushered Chloe in, closed the door and gently guided her over to sofa. As he did so, he tried to get in touch with how he felt about all of this.

"What happened?"

"Best friends, you just can't trust them," she said regaining her composure a little. Tom didn't say anything; he didn't want to jump to the wrong conclusion.

"Katrina, she was always jealous of us, always wanting to come round for no real reason." Tom sat down on the other sofa. He wanted to keep a healthy distance; his emotional barriers were up high. He knew exactly what that felt like. For your trust to be shattered by your best friend and the hurt, like that person had reached inside of you, grabbed hold of your heart and squeezed the life out of it. Leaving you feeling betrayed and unsure of yourself.

"Hmm," she said half laughing, half crying, "somehow, someone left a picture on my screen saver. Rick denies it of course but then why would he put it on there? Anyway it was a picture of her and him, kissing. He was only wearing a towel, my towel. Can you believe that? What sort of a sick person does something like that?"

"Really, imagine that. What sort of a person?" echoed Tom as he realised the irony of the whole episode.

"He claimed it was some sort of practical joke, that someone had tampered with the photograph and, for a moment, just for a split second, I almost believed him. He said I was paranoid. Me the most trusting person on the planet, paranoid. But then I took a deep breath and there was this smell. The bedroom smelt of her, her perfume. Chanel. And I think that, subconsciously, I'd had my suspicions for a while but I just chose to ignore them. And then I thought, there's only ever been one person that's really cared about me, you know. Knows the true person that I really am. Do you think I could have a drink?"

"What do you want?" Tom answered, without thinking. It had only taken a few moments for him to slip back into his old habits.

"A lemon tea would be nice. As long as you've got real lemons of course. Can't stand that instant stuff."

"No problem. A shot of something a bit stronger in there, just to help you relax?"

"You see Tom, you know me so well," she said giving him that smile. He quickly trotted off to the kitchen and obediently made the drinks with all the care and devotion of someone dedicated to the one purpose that makes their life worthwhile. By the time he'd got back, Chloe had made herself comfortable. Her jacket was draped over one of the dining room chairs and she'd spread herself out on the sofa, lying on her side with her legs up, with the remote control in her hand. Tom carefully placed the lemon tea on a coaster on the coffee table and then sat down in the small space at the end of the sofa, by her feet. Chloe put the remote control on the sofa and began to twist locks of her long blond hair around her index finger.

"Tom," she said turning to face him. "I realise that I've made a terrible mistake. Do you think that you can ever forgive me?" Then like a true sales woman, who'd had a lifetime of getting her own way and wrapping men around her finger, like she was wrapping her hair, Chloe gave him her best pitch.

"I know it sounds, well, it's out of the blue but, I realise now that after all that's happened, well I'm just going come right out and say it. It's you that I care about Tom. It always has been, all along. I've just never realised it before. You're my rock. The one that's always been there to pick up the pieces. To guide me to shore during troubled waters. We're like strawberries and cream; we were made for each other. And well I know I've hurt you but I also know that I can make it better. It can be like the old days, like we used to be, inseparable. What do you say?"

"Well it's all a bit sudden really. You only told me a few days ago that you were marrying someone else, who turned out to be my best friend."

"Yes but that was a mistake, a mistake, can't you see that? It was all a terrible mistake."

"I need some time Chloe."

"Ok, look I've got an idea. Just listen to this. You don't have to say yes straight away, but on the way over I picked up some brochures, they're in my bag and well I thought we could go away for a week. Somewhere where the weather's a bit better. Somewhere that meant something to us. Help rekindle the old flame."

"Well, yeah I guess we could do something. I do need a holiday that's for sure."

"Great, no pressure, just a week away, you and me, a bit of quality time together."

"Ok, so where? Where did you have in mind?"

"I thought, Ibiza. Oh Tom it would be wonderful. Do you remember what a great holiday we had? Didn't we just have the best time?"

This was it for Tom, the straw that broke the camel's back. It was as if Chloe had uttered the password that triggers the brainwashed mild mannered accountant to turn into a ruthless killing machine. At first he didn't know what to do. He stayed still, trying to get in touch with his emotions. Then he thought of his granddad. It made him feel sad and he began to miss him. Through this process he was able to tap into the disappointment and hurt Chloe had made him feel by leaving him on his own in the holiday apartment.

"I hated the holiday in Ibiza," he eventually said in a calm voice, fully expecting a torrent of abuse to come forth from Chloe's lips.

"I, I didn't know that," she replied, genuinely looking surprised and a little perplexed.

"Why would you? It's like you said when we met up you didn't know I liked wearing green jumpers. You didn't know that I love Christmas and, and, you didn't know my sister was dead."

"Rebecca's dead. Oh my God."

"Not Rebecca, Jessica."

"Who's Jessica?"

"My other sister. When I was young. She died in a, in a car accident."

"You never told me that," Chloe said looking put out.

"That's because we only ever talked about you." But as soon as he said it, Tom regretted being so hurtful.

"Well that's my point. If we go on holiday we can get to know each other better."

"I'm not sure it's what I want."

"Come on. I'm sure it is, a nice time, you and me, relaxing by the pool, soaking up the rays."

Tom still wasn't convinced, so Chloe changed her approach and suddenly began to cry.

"What's wrong?" Tom asked immediately being drawn in. He moved a bit closer to try and comfort her.

"I just, need to relax. I'm so stressed at the moment," she said dabbing away the tears as they materialised.

"We could relax together, here in London if you want."

"It's not what I want," and like Dr Jykell her mood changed again. In a matter of minutes Tom had seen her go from being nice, to sobbing her heart out, to being aggressive, just because she wasn't getting her own way. He stood up and went to walk out of the lounge.

"Where are you going?" asked Chloe, in a tone that made Tom feel she was unsure of what was going on. It was the voice of someone losing control.

"I'm going to the toilet."

"Well hurry back."

"Christ I can't even take a leak on my own," Tom said under his breath while his back was turned.

"What was that?"

"Nothing, don't worry about it" he replied. As soon as he got to the toilet, he twisted the tap on and splashed his face with freezing cold water. He stood up and stared in the mirror. Looking back at him were his mother's eyes. A permanent glint of disappointment radiated out of them.

"What am I doing?" And then it hit him. The hurt of being left alone in his flat for the last year. The hurt of being left alone in Ibiza. The hurt of losing his sister. The hurt of his best friend sleeping with his girlfriend. The feeling quickly overwhelmed him but by the same token it sobered him up. It made him come to his senses and like the flick of a switch, something changed inside of him and he realised he couldn't do this anymore. However much he hated upsetting people, he couldn't live his life with someone that was capable of doing the things that Chloe had done to him.

He splashed some more water onto his face, wiped it on the towel that was on the radiator next to the sink and took a deep breath. When he came back into the living room, he found that Chloe had poured herself a glass of milk and had turned the TV on.

"You've got to see this bit," she said laughing, "this is really really funny. Look, watch where the squirrel goes," she said gesturing at the TV with her hand. Her mood change was nothing short of miraculous. Tom didn't bother sitting down this time but chose to walk in front of the TV.

"Tom, Tom what are you doing?" Then in one smooth motion he grabbed hold of the remote control which was on top of the coffee table, pointed it at the TV behind him and switched it off.

"Tom, look I know it's difficult for you at the moment…" Tom found himself raising his hand just like Den would have done.

"No Chloe, this time it's my turn to speak."

"Come on then," she said folding her arms.

"I can't, I can't do this. I need to be sure that the person closest to me, the one that I would like to spend the rest of my life with, to dress the Christmas tree with, go to my favourite restaurant with, our favourite restaurant, relax in front of the TV with, that she loves me unconditionally, and I'm just not sure that you're that person."

"But I…"

"No, please let me finish," Tom said holding up his hand again and taking a deep breath. "I haven't come to this decision lightly and there are several reasons why I can't do this. It's not just about you going behind my back with my best friend, it's everything. Do you know I can't remember a single present that you've ever brought me, not one; birthdays, Christmas or Valentines or just a spur of the moment thing? You never told me how much I light you up. I haven't got a clue if I'm special to you or not; that the world's a better place because I'm in it with you. I've never heard you talk highly of me to other people, that I've done things that make you happy or made you feel special. You never made me feel secure. Do you know almost from day one I was looking over my shoulder, wondering who was going to catch your eye? Constantly being compared to other people, who had more money or better houses or were funnier or more charming than I was. Then, when I needed you the most, like in Ibiza, when I was ill and tired and sad, you weren't there for me. You were off having a better time. And when something special for me came up, like decorating the Christmas tree, you forgot to turn up, too busy doing your own thing. When you used to tell me you loved me, it never meant anything. You never said it with any passion or joy or backed it up with real emotion. And when I asked you for money, when I really needed it just a few days ago, you wouldn't do it. I'd give you the shirt off my back, do you know that? But you, you wouldn't give me the change in your purse. The little things that I love about you, like your hooked nose and the way you always pronounce your 'Ss' or when you wash your hands three times and the fact that you love Celine Dion and Jethro Tull. The fact that you were forever losing your keys. Yet all my faults just endlessly annoyed you. My indecisiveness, my overuse of the word 'actually,' my punctuality or my, my insistence on folding up my clothes and neatly placing them in a pile, drove you mad, even though I never asked you to tidy up the mess that you always left behind. Your constant criticism of people who care about me, like my sister and my grand-dad. And rather than help me build better relationships with people, it was like your goal was to destroy them and isolate me. Whenever it was time to go and see my friends or my family you were struck down by some mysterious illness. In fact the only person you got on with was my mum and that about sums the problem up. And finally, finally, because I really think that this is evidence enough but just the fact that I never appear to be in your thoughts in a good way is too much for me." Chloe sat on the sofa, her arms still folded with a stern expression on her face. Tom waited for her to say something.

"You're, you're such a loser. I'm the best thing that ever happened to you, do you know that? If I was to the walk out of that door now I'm never coming back. Do you realise that?"

Tom suddenly had a moment of self doubt. He wondered whether he was doing the right thing, but then he remembered that he just wanted to be happy. One thing was for sure, he'd never felt that way when he was with Chloe. Sometimes in life, Tom's granddad used to say, you have to let go of things to know if they are truly for you. Tear all the layers away to find out who you really are and what you really want.

"If you can't change or you don't want to change, Chloe, I do understand. I don't want you to pretend to be someone that you're not."

"I thought you loved me."

"I do. The problem is that I don't think you love me."

"I've had enough of this," she said getting up off the sofa. "This is your last chance."

"Last chance for what?"

"Whatever," she said throwing her right arm in the air. She grabbed hold of her handbag and coat and then walked out the front door, not without pausing to show Tom the hurt expression on her face. Tom looked back but said nothing. As soon as she'd gone he got up and shut the door behind her. He then slowly made his way back to the sofa, before collapsing onto it. But rather than feeling upset or lost or depressed, Tom felt liberated, as if a large weight had been lifted off his shoulders. Rather than thinking about Chloe anymore and what she was doing or what she wanted, he could finally focus on himself.

He looked at the Christmas tree in the corner of his flat. Its branches had started to drop a little and the needles had begun to fall onto the carpet. Then it dawned on him that it would soon be the twelfth night.

Tom's granddad was very superstitious and there was no way he would have broken that tradition. So even though Tom was mentally and emotionally drained, he pulled himself up off the sofa, went to the cupboard in the spare room and pulled out two boxes full of scrunched up tissue paper. He brought them back into the lounge and placed them on the coffee table. The first thing that he laid eyes on was the Father Christmas that his grandmother had made for him all those years ago. He carefully unhooked it from the tree and held it in his hands. It didn't take long for the memories to come flooding back.

"Tom look what grandma has made," said Albert, opening up the old shoe box. Tom had just turned five years old. He remembered peering up at his granddad wondering if the day could get any better after eating and drinking a seemingly endless stream of treats. Albert bent down and placed the shoe box in front of him and then lifted the lid off. Inside was a hand stitched Father Christmas, his beard made out of white cloth, his red coat made out of felt, his eyes were tiny brown buttons and his legs were filled like a bean bag.

"That's lovely," Tom said his eyes the size of gold fish bowls. "Can I hold it?"

"Of course you can, it's for you."

"It's for me? But it's not Christmas yet."

"We know but it's just that you've been such a good boy."

"Thanks. Thanks grandma, thanks granddad," and he beckoned his grandma over and grabbed hold of both of them and pulled them in as tightly as he could.

"Da…da da dah…da da dah…der der der der derh…da…da da dah…da da dah…der der der der derh," went Tom's mobile phone. He quickly put his Father Christmas down on the coffee table next to the boxes and embarked on a frantic hunt for his phone, which wasn't anywhere in sight.

"Come on, come on, where are you?" he said as he started randomly lifting cushions up. He paused, looked up and saw his jacket on the floor behind the sofa. Running round he lunged for the inside pocket and felt something solid.

"Hello, hello."

"Hello Tom, expecting someone important," came a woman's voice. For a split second he thought it might be Chloe. Outside with a special Christmas present. A butcher's knife to cut him into little pieces.

"Who's that?"

"Has it really been that long?"

"Rebecca," Tom said feeling so relieved he started to laugh.

"What's so funny?"

"Oh nothing, it's more hysterical laughter really, I've just had Chloe round."

"Really does she need to borrow some more money?"

"Not exactly, no."

"Anyway forget about her, she's old hat, yesterday's news. Time to move it on up, I'm movin' on up...," Rebecca started singing down the phone.

"Yeah, you know I think you could be right."

"Damn sure I'm right and speaking of moving on, guess who phoned me today?"

"Errh, Madonna phoned up to see if she could adopt you."

"Nope, not even warm."

"President Bush called to ask how to spell the word sorry."

"Way way off."

"Elvis Presley wanted to take you out for a burger."

"Not funny. Look we're going to be here all day. I'll give you a clue."

"Ok, give me a clue."

"Earmuffs."

"Big ears."

"No it's not word association."

"Oh I know, Angela."

"That's right and guess what else."

"I don't know, what else?"

"She's free tomorrow night."

EPILOGUE
Sometimes in life, you get what you want

"Daddy, mummy says you need to hurry up," said the little girl, whilst brushing her long, dark hair away from her face. She looked tiny standing in the middle of the large Victorian lounge, with its high ceilings.

"Ok Eva, I'll be with you in a minute."

"Mummy says that it starts at four thirty and it's four o'clock now."

"Don't worry, I promise we won't miss a thing."

Eva turned round and ran back out of the room. Tom could hear her voice in the distance, relaying the news to her mum. He was sitting at a beautiful oak desk, which had drawers either side, fiddling with the mouse of his black laptop, using it to click on the latest e-mail he'd just received.

The results of the auction are as follows:
Bid number: 31
Final price: £3,826

Bid winner: Mr H.G. Payne, Tunbridge Wells, Kent
Deposit: £800

"Good, good, good," he said to himself closing down the systems on his laptop and clicking the lid shut. He got up from his leather seat and as he walked through to the hallway called out "Right kids, have you got everything?" Eva was standing in front of him dressed in a pink coat, matching hat and scarf and Wellington boots.

"Dad, it's not us that needs to get ready."

"Yes, come on dad," said a fresh faced looking Angela, who'd just entered the hallway, giving him a quick squeeze on his shoulder. "We don't want to miss a thing," she whispered in his ear. "You've bigged it up so much the kids haven't been able to sleep properly for the last two nights."

"Nothing to do with it being Christmas Eve then," he replied smiling.

"Just get your jacket on and let's get going."

"Where's Charlie?" Tom asked as he looked up at Angela. She smiled and placed her index finger up to the front of her month. Tom took the hint and fell silent. He was just able to hear the gentle sound of a child's voice coming from one of the bedrooms,

"…silent night, holy night, all is clear, all is bright…"

"He's been practicing for the last week," explained Angela.

"Ok, ok, I get the hint." Tom quickly went back into the lounge and put his laptop away in the bottom drawer of his desk. He then grabbed his jacket, scarf and hat from the bedroom. On the way back out to the hallway he was met with three expectant faces.

"Come on dad," the two kids said in unison.

"Right. God you lot take ages to get ready. If we don't hurry it will all be over soon." No one fell for it, although Eva did give her dad a rather disapproving look. As soon as Tom opened the front door, the kids ran down the stone steps and out onto the snow covered gravel driveway.

"Stay where I can see you," shouted Angela. She then promptly turned her attention back to Tom. "I hope for your sake the donkey's not sick this year," she said quietly while putting her hand through the hole he'd made with his arm.

"We're done for if he is."

"You don't know, it could be a she donkey."

"Let's hope so, because then she'll probably be late."

"Errh, pot-kettle," Angela said with a grin on her face.

As they got to the end of the road, the heath opened up in front of them. The sun was disappearing over the horizon, and on such a clear night it illuminated their path, all the way down to Blackheath Village. It was so atmospheric walking in such a wide open space in the middle of London. especially with the snow covering the grass. Sometimes when Tom made this trip he felt like he was on top of the world. Small and insignificant compared to nature and the enormous expanse of sky above him. The clouds looked large and exaggerated, like staring up through a gigantic magnifying glass.

Eva and Charlie chased each other along the path that ran through the middle of the heath. Charlie stopped to bend down and grab hold of some snow, patting it into a ball, before standing back up and chasing after his sister.

"Don't you ever wonder what would have happened if I'd never knocked you over on the ice rink?"

"I try not to think about it," replied Angela.

"Really, why's that?"

"Because I'm so happy, like I never thought I could be and I realise that I've got everything I've ever wanted. You and the kids, our little family unit."

"Yeah our little family," Tom said smiling. They soon reached the top of the village and then made their way down the hill, where a crowd of expectant people, mainly parents with their children, had gathered holding paper cups of coffee and moving around on the spot to keep their feet warm.

"Da…da da dah…da da dah…der der der der derh…da…da da dah…da da dah…der der der der derh…"

"When are you going to change that ringtone?" Asked Angela.

"What, you can never get tired of a classic like the 'Eye of the Tiger'…Rocky Balboa…ehh Adrian," Tom said, doing a rather poor impression of Sylvester Stallone while bouncing on the spot and pretending to punch the air. That was until he remembered someone was on the end of the line. He flicked open his mobile phone.

"Hello, Tom."

"Who's that?"

"Turn to your right."

"Ok."

"Bit further." As Tom slowly moved round, he recognised his friend wearing one of those pointed brightly coloured woolly hats with flaps that cover your ears, holding his hand up.

"Dennis, hello mate. I didn't think you were coming."

"Oh no I was just pulling your leg. Wouldn't miss it for the world. Little Jenny loves it. Hasn't stopped going on about it all week. Anyway I'm going to get off the phone, you'll be able to hear me soon."

"Hi Angela," Den said, leaning forward to kiss her on the cheek.

"Hi Den, hi Yvonne, been here long?" asked Tom.

"Oh about half an hour, I think Den is more excited than Jenny," replied Yvonne.

"Boys didn't fancy it?" asked Tom.

"No they're a bit old for it now. Off round their friend's house for a night of computer games."

"Any sign yet?" asked Angela.

"We overheard someone saying that they're not far away now," said Yvonne.

"Thank heaven for that, we were worried we might've missed it."

"Alright Yvonne?" asked Tom.

"Yes I am. I got that job I was telling you about, nursery school teacher."

"Congratulations," Tom and Angela said together.

"Thanks for the reference."

"No worries," replied Tom. "Got some good news for you mate."

"What's that, have I won the Pools?"

"Listen dad," interrupted Eva, grabbing hold of Tom's arm. On her command they all stopped talking. In the distance the faint sound of a brass band could be heard; the notes to the Christmas hymn Silent Night gliding through the air. The crowd that had gathered were restless, as expectations of the arrival of the main event grew stronger. Then round the corner, at the bottom of Blackheath Village, a donkey could be seen led by a teenage boy, wearing a brown cloak, with a white cloth wrapped around his head. He was walking to the left of the donkey. In his right hand he was carrying a wooden staff and had the reins in the other. Sitting on the donkey was a girl wearing similar clothes. Either side of them were some people carrying a banner which read "United Churches of Blackheath."

"Look dad, look," said Charlie tugging at Tom's other sleeve. Following close behind the donkey was a brass band, made up of musicians of all ages. They walked in loose formation, stopping just past the train station at the bottom of Blackheath Village to finish the tune they were playing. It gave the people who'd been following them time to catch up. The man in front of the brass band carrying the trombone then counted them in and they began playing Good King Wenceslas. They then resumed their journey up the hill towards the heath. Once the short procession had walked past them, Den, Yvonne, Tom, Angela and their children mingled in with the crowd, following the brass band towards All Saints Church. Eva grabbed hold of her dad's hand, while Charlie held onto his mother's. When they reached the top, the brass band finished off the hymn they were playing and then arranged themselves on the steps of the church. Spotlights lit up the church and parts of the congregation.

"So what's the good news then," Den asked as soon as he managed to catch up with Tom in front of the church.

"You, my friend, have sold another painting and guess what?"

"You had to give it away?"

"Nope, not even close. There were three main bidders who between them pushed the price up past £3,800 pounds."

"Nearly four grand, I don't know what to say."

"Don't have to say anything. Making quite a name for yourself apparently."

"God moves in mysterious ways," Den said.

"You deserve it mate. In fact, no one deserves it more than you do."

"Yvonne, pack your bags. You know that trip to Italy, it's as good as booked."

"It's a bit cold to go now Denny."

"You know what I mean, for the summer."

"Are you serious?" Yvonne said looking at Tom for some sort of confirmation.

"When have I let you down," replied Den. "Actually don't answer that." As Den and Tom were talking, they tried to keep their voices down because the vicar was saying a few words.

"Do you know my life's gone from strength to strength since that day?"

"Since what day?"

"Since the day you said we could all share the money."

"Thanks for being honest enough to give it back. Didn't know you and Jack had it in you," Tom said smiling. "You should be proud of yourself, you did the right thing. It provided the money I needed to set up my Internet business and for you to concentrate on your painting. Just to think that a few years ago it would have taken months to sell one of your paintings and we would have been lucky to get two hundred pounds. Now they go in a few days and fetch nearly twenty times that amount."

"Thanks," said Den patting Tom on the shoulder.

"No, thank you mate. Merry Christmas."

"Merry Christmas back at you."

"How is Jack by the way?" asked Tom.

"He is now in the process of setting up his third Nick-Nack shop."

"Blimey, who'd have believed it. Good for him."

It was at this point of the proceedings that the vicar signalled to the brass band for them to start playing. The notes of the carol 'The Twelve Days of Christmas' filled the air and everyone started to sing.

"On the first day of Christmas my true love sent to me, a partridge in a pear tree."

"On the second day of Christmas my true love sent to me…."

"….two turtle doves…and a partridge in a pear tree."

"On the third day of Christmas my true love sent to me…."

At this point Tom turned his attention away from the brass band and gazed down at his daughter Eva, who was holding her song sheet tightly with both hands. Next to her stood Charlie, clutching a small tin lantern in his right hand. They were singing their hearts out, and just for a split second, Tom thought she looked like his sister Jessica. Eva sensed that her father was looking at her and glanced up.

"I love you dad," she said smiling.

"I love you too," replied Tom. She then kissed the palm of her glove and blew him a kiss. Tom acted as if the kiss was an illusive butterfly, fluttering around his head, almost getting away before he finally caught it in his hand. He then gestured to Eva that he was putting it in his jacket pocket. Tom returned the imaginary kiss with one of his own. After catching it in her glove and pretending to do the same, Eva said grinning from ear to ear, "This is the best Christmas present ever."

With a lump in his throat Tom replied, "Yes it is. It's the best Christmas present ever."